STONE ARCH BOOKS
a capstone imprint

STONE ARCH BOOKS™
Published in 2014
A Capstone Imprint
1710 Roe Crest Drive
North Mankato, MN 56003
www.capstonepub.com

Originally published by DC Comics in the U.S. in single magazine form as Teen Titans GO! #3.

DC Comics
1700 Broadway, New York, NY 10019
A Warner Bros. Entertainment Company

Cataloging-in-Publication Data is available at the Library of Congress website:
ISBN: 978-1-4342-6467-1 (library binding)

Summary: Cyborg learns the difference between being cool and lame as Cinderblock attempts to destroy Jump City!

STONE ARCH BOOKS
Ashley C. Andersen Zantop *Publisher*
Michael Dahl *Editorial Director*
Sean Tulien *Editor*
Heather Kindseth *Creative Director*
Alison Thiele *Designer*
Kathy McColley *Production Specialist*

DC COMICS
Kristy Quinn Original U.S. Editor

Printed in the United States of America in Stevens Point, Wisconsin.
072014 008385R

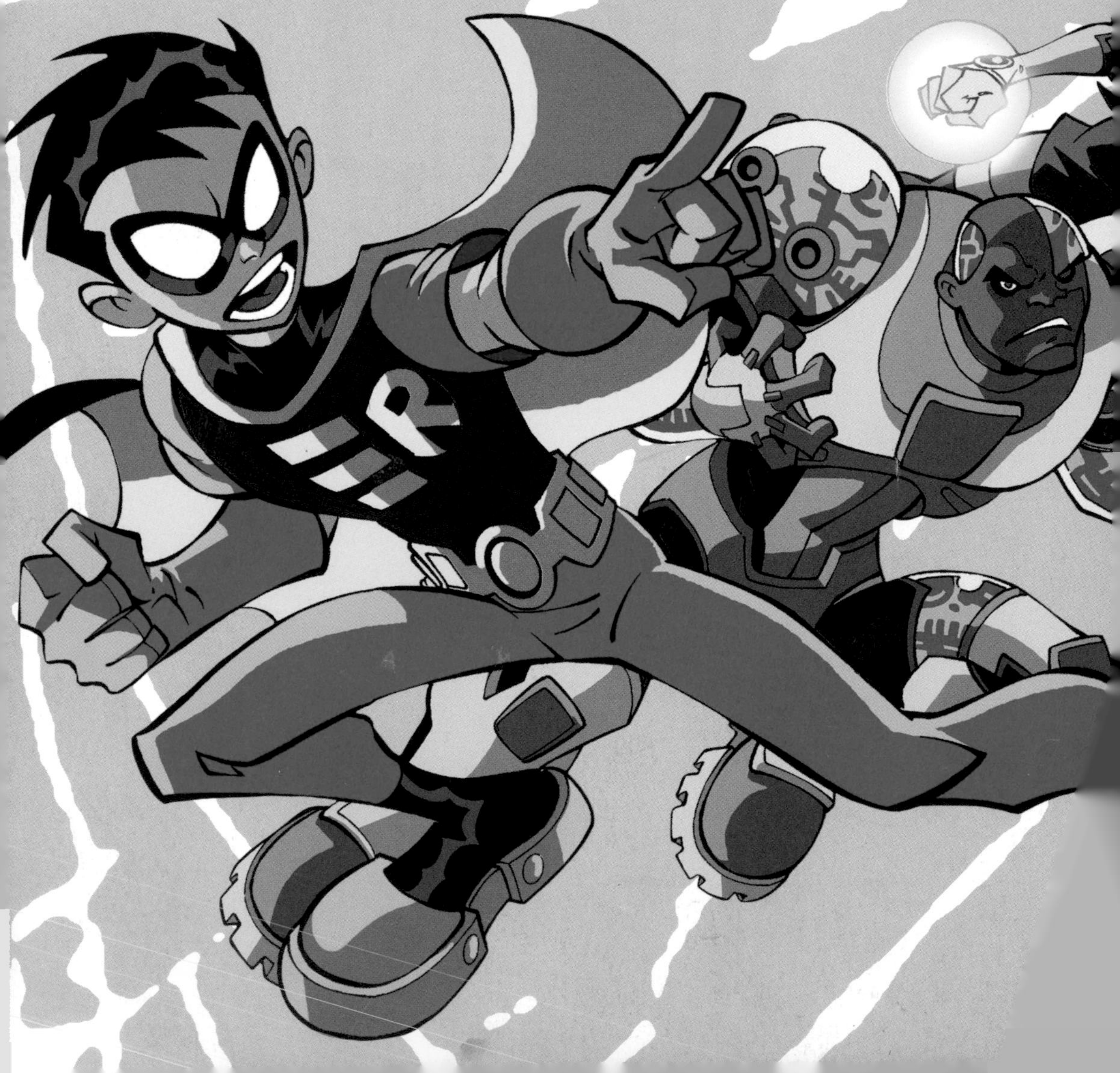
R

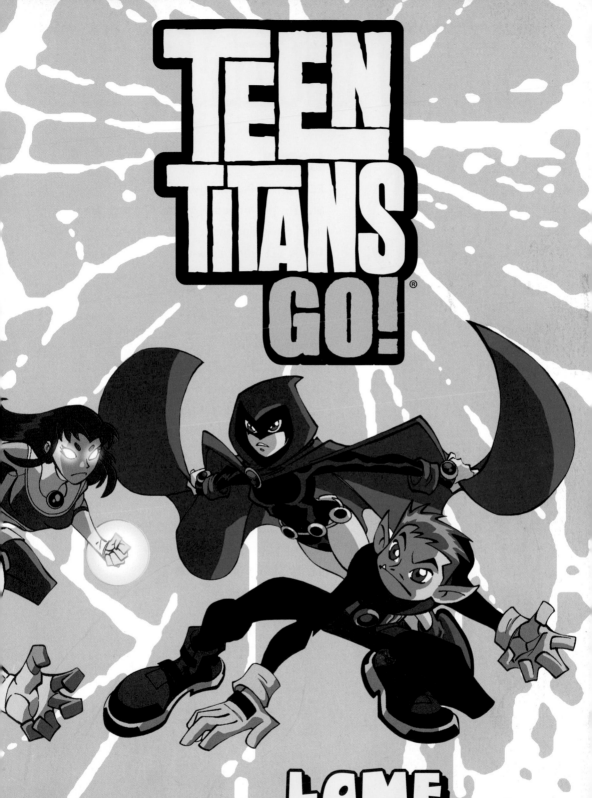

TEEN TITANS GO!®

LAME

J. Torres	writer
Tim Smith 3 & Lary Stucker	artists
Brad Anderson	colorist
Jared K. Fletcher	letterer

TEEN TITANS GO!

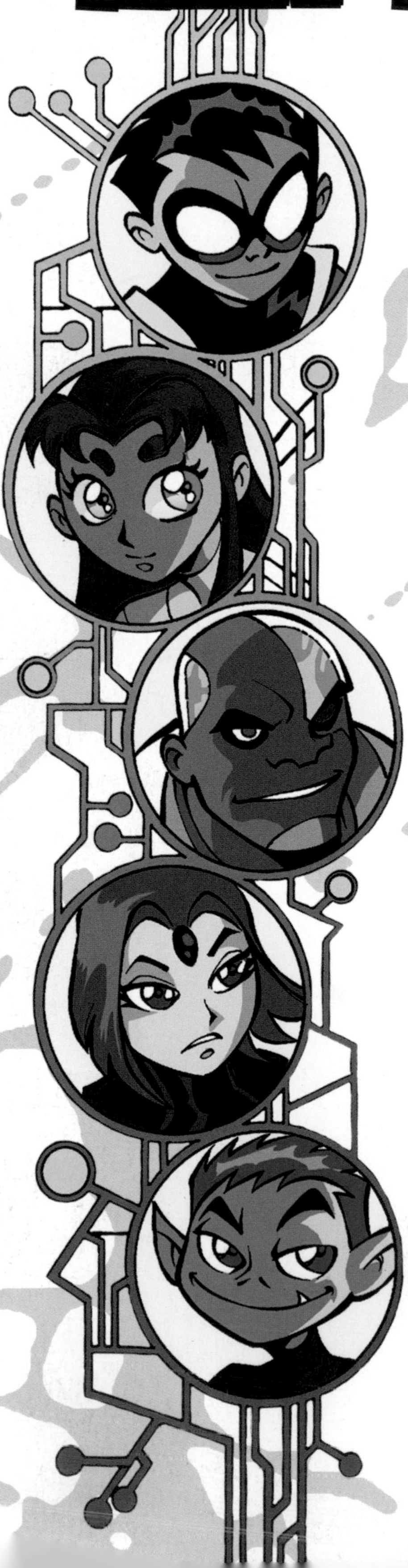

ROBIN

REAL NAME: Dick Grayson

BIO: The perfectionist leader of the group has one main complaint about his teammates: the other Titans just won't do what he says. As the partner of Batman, Robin is a talented acrobat, martial artist, and hacker.

STARFIRE

REAL NAME: Princess Koriand'r

BIO: Formerly a warrior Princess of the now-destroyed planet Tamaran, Starfire found a new home on Earth, and a new family in the Teen Titans.

CYBORG

REAL NAME: Victor Stone

BIO: Cyborg is a laid-back half teen, half robot who's more interested in eating pizza and playing video games than fighting crime.

RAVEN

REAL NAME: Raven

BIO: Raven is an Azarathian empath who can teleport and control her "soul-self," which can fight physically as well as act as Raven's eyes and ears away from her body.

BEAST BOY

REAL NAME: Garfield Logan

BIO: Beast Boy is Cyborg's best bud. He's a slightly dim but lovable loafer who can transform into all sorts of animals [when he's not too busy eating burritos and watching TV]. He's also a vegetarian.

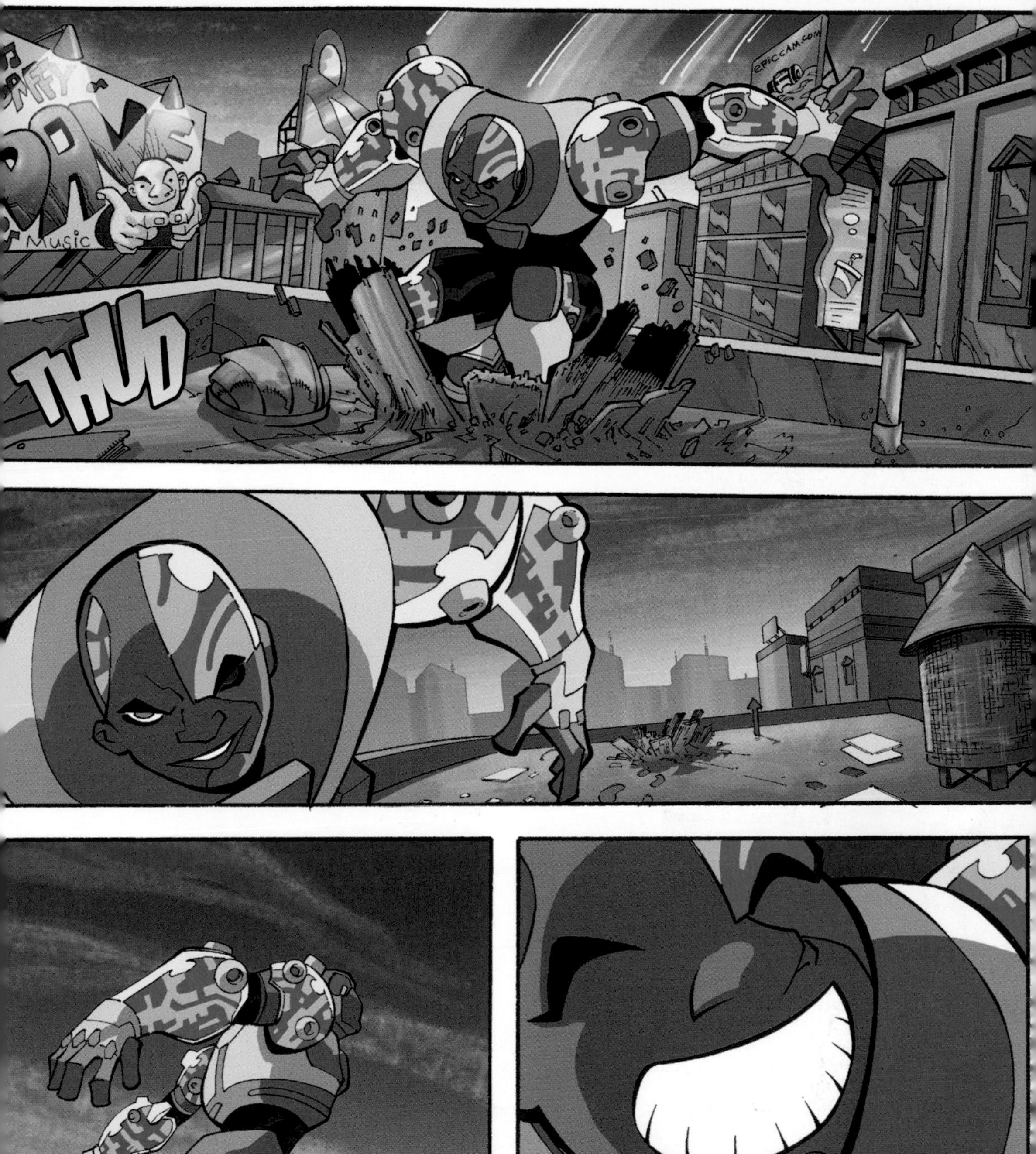
Music
epiccam.com
THUD
OH, YEAH...

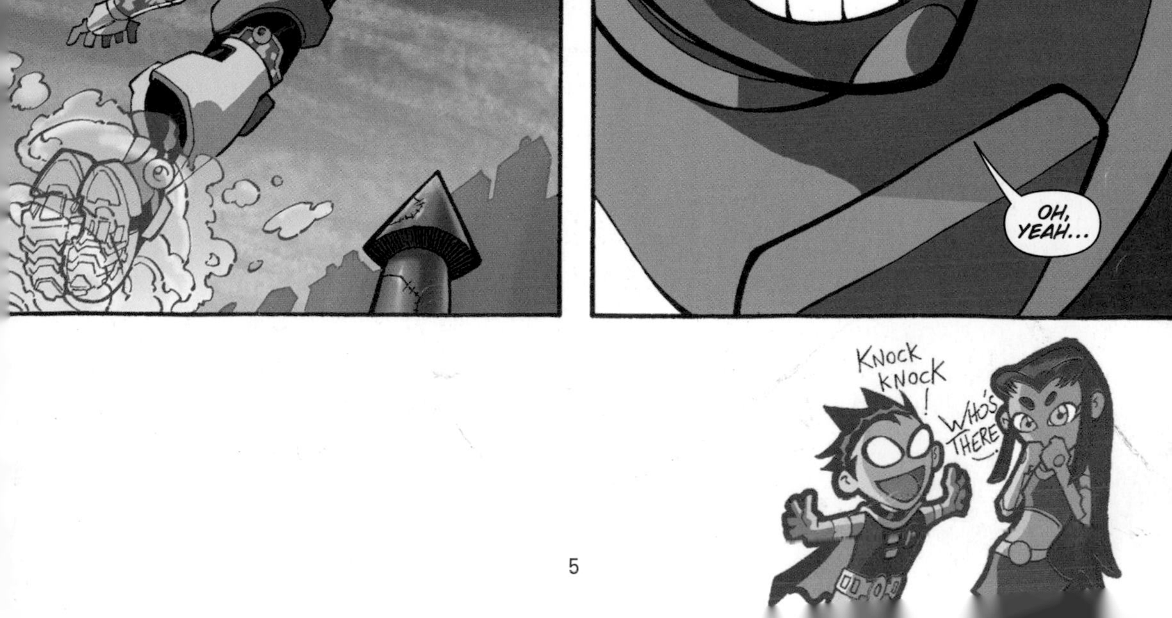
KNOCK KNOCK!
WHO'S THERE?

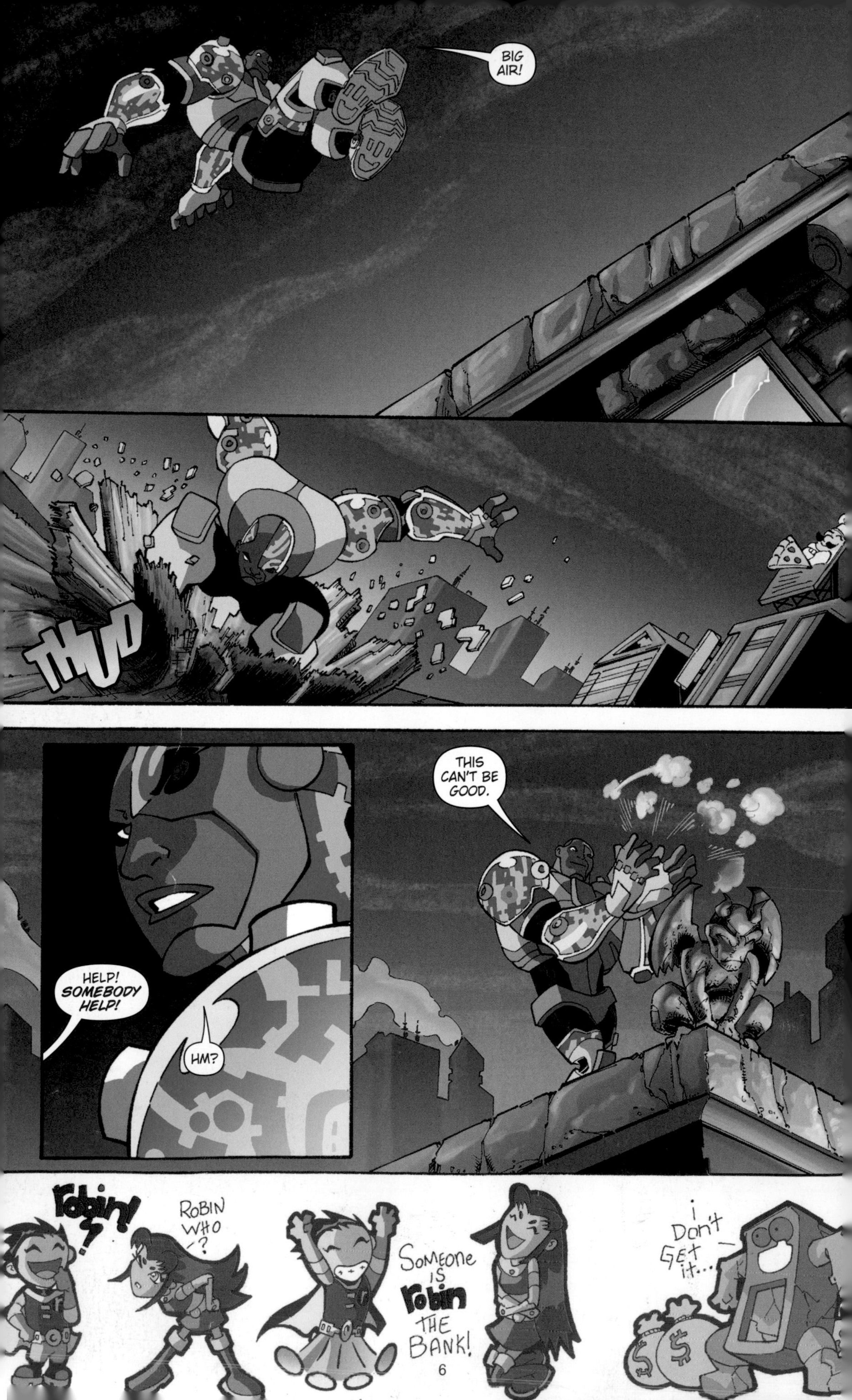

BIG AIR!
THUD
HELP! SOMEBODY HELP!
HM?
THIS CAN'T BE GOOD.
robin!
ROBIN WHO-?
Someone is robin the Bank!
i Don't Get it...

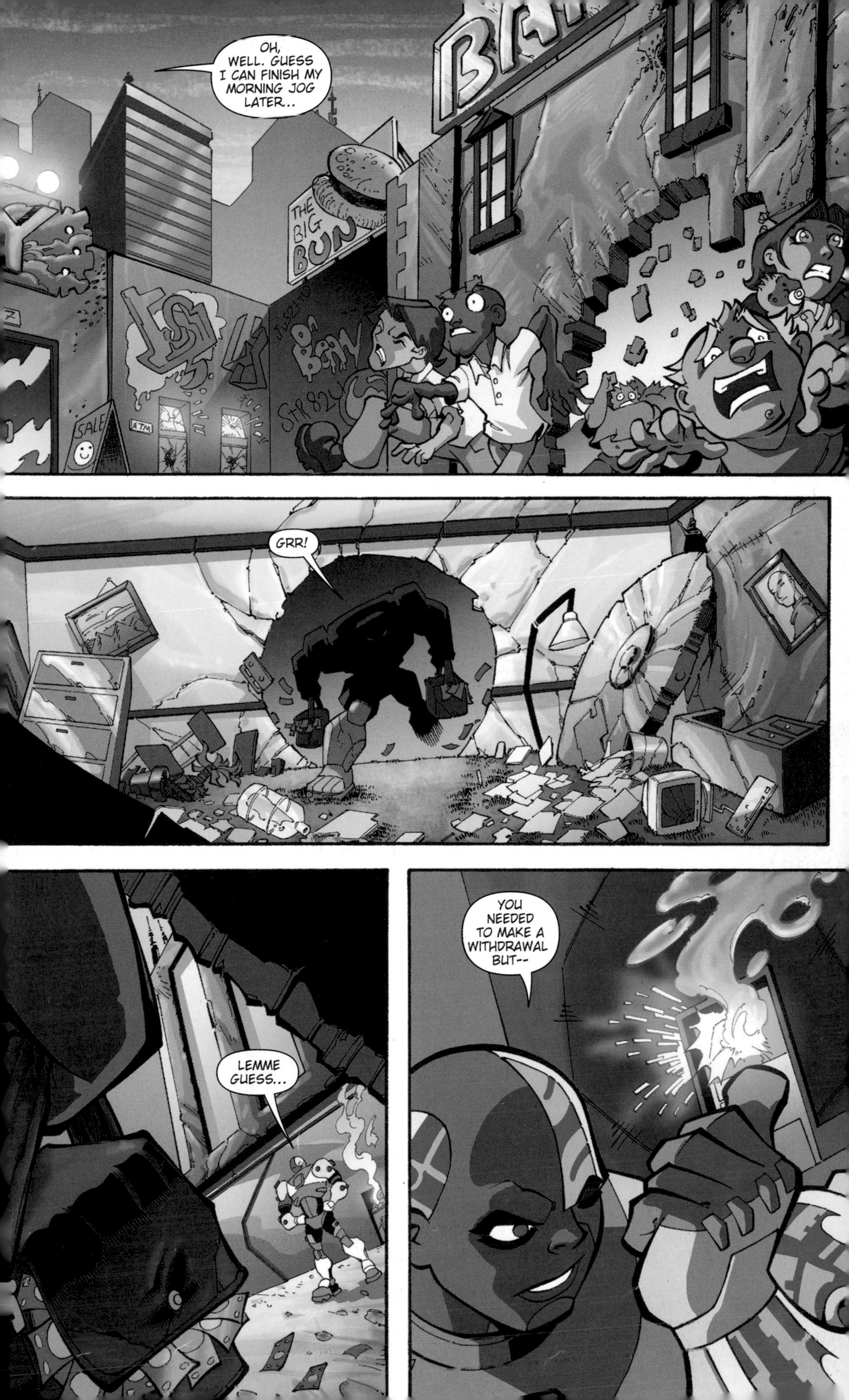
OH, WELL. GUESS I CAN FINISH MY MORNING JOG LATER...
THE BIG BUN
SALE
ATM
GRR!
LEMME GUESS...
YOU NEEDED TO MAKE A WITHDRAWAL BUT--

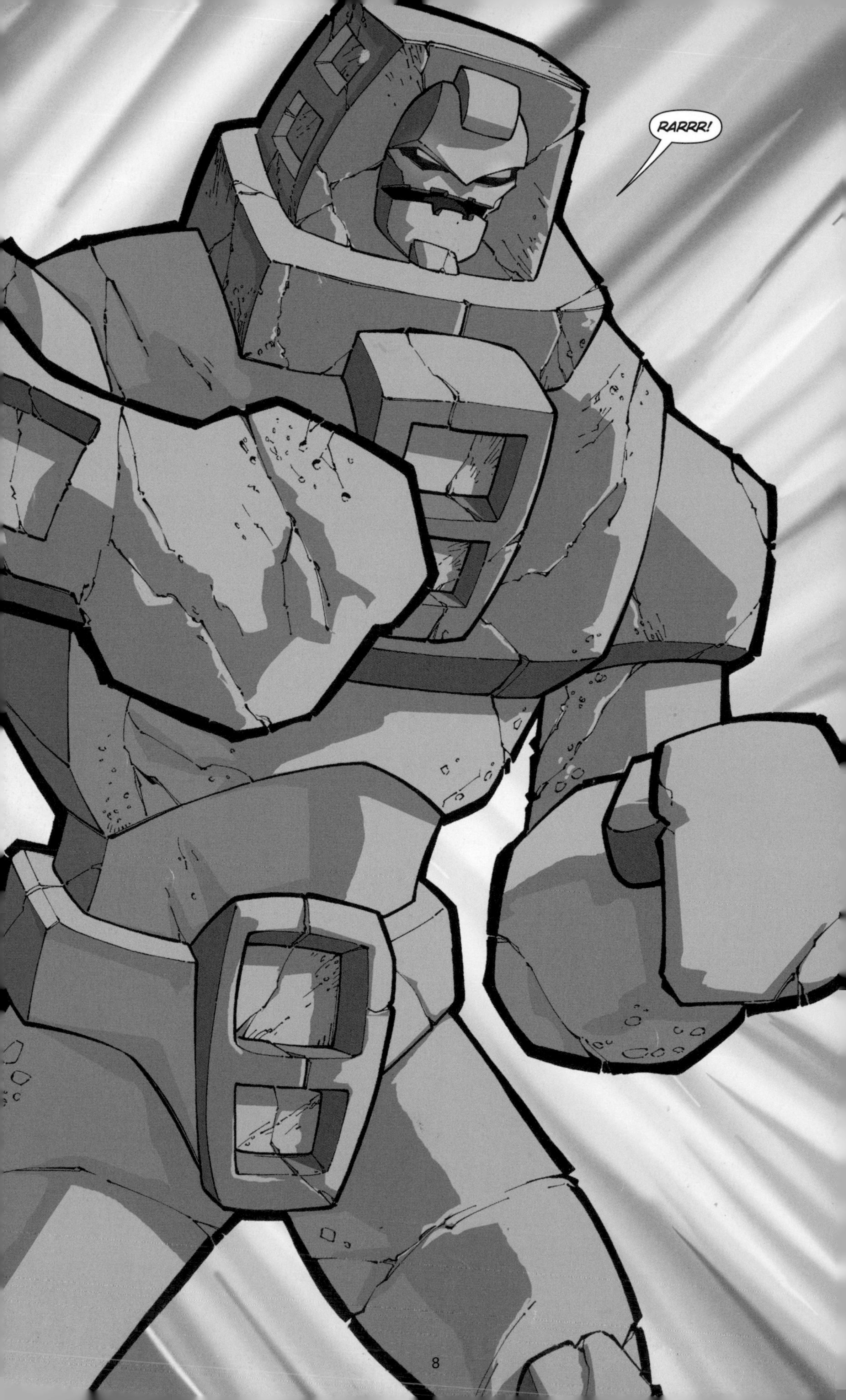
RARRR!

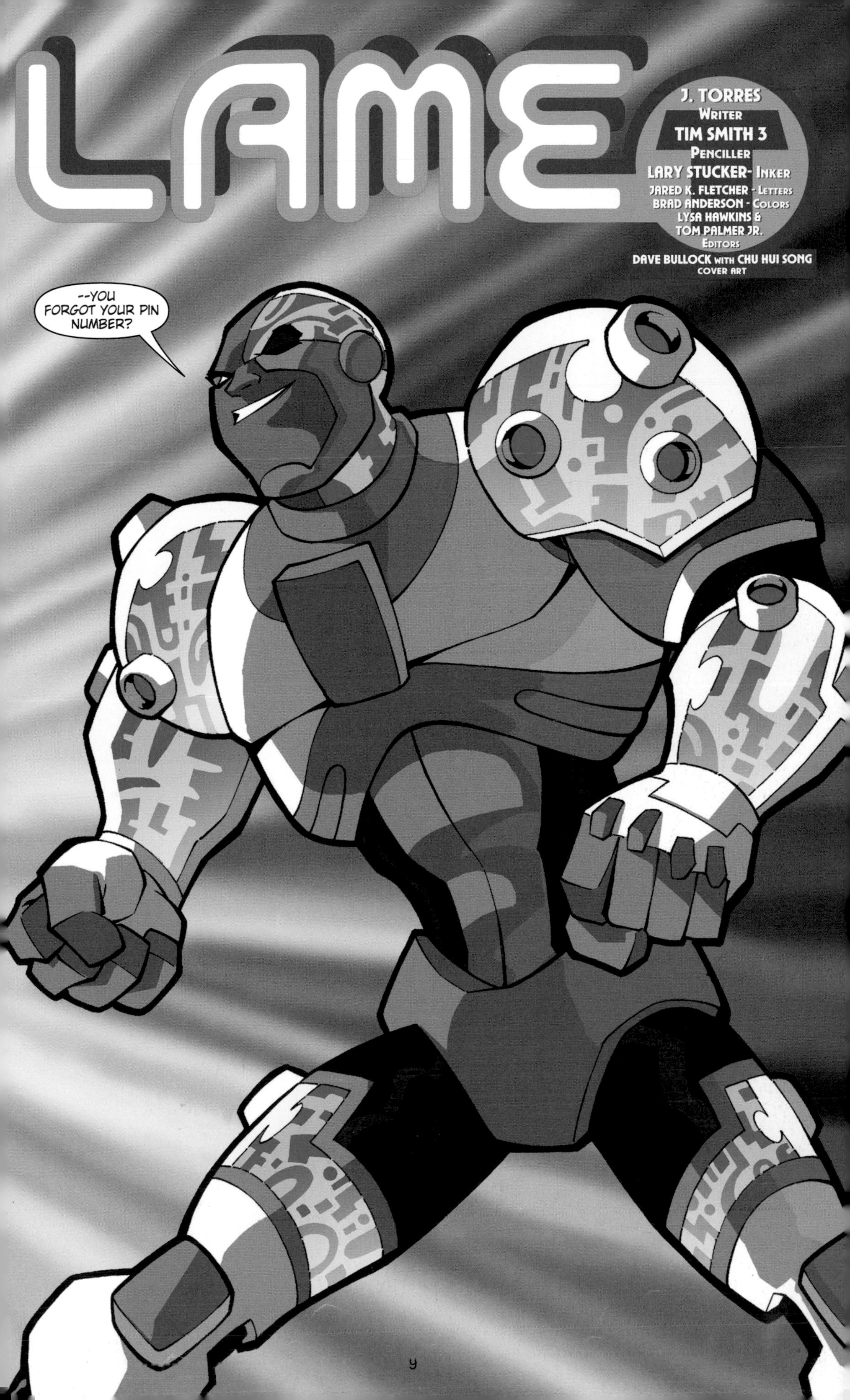
LAME
J. TORRES
WRITER
TIM SMITH 3
PENCILLER
LARY STUCKER- INKER
JARED K. FLETCHER - LETTERS
BRAD ANDERSON - COLORS
LYSA HAWKINS &
TOM PALMER JR.
EDITORS
DAVE BULLOCK WITH CHU HUI SONG
COVER ART
--YOU FORGOT YOUR PIN NUMBER?

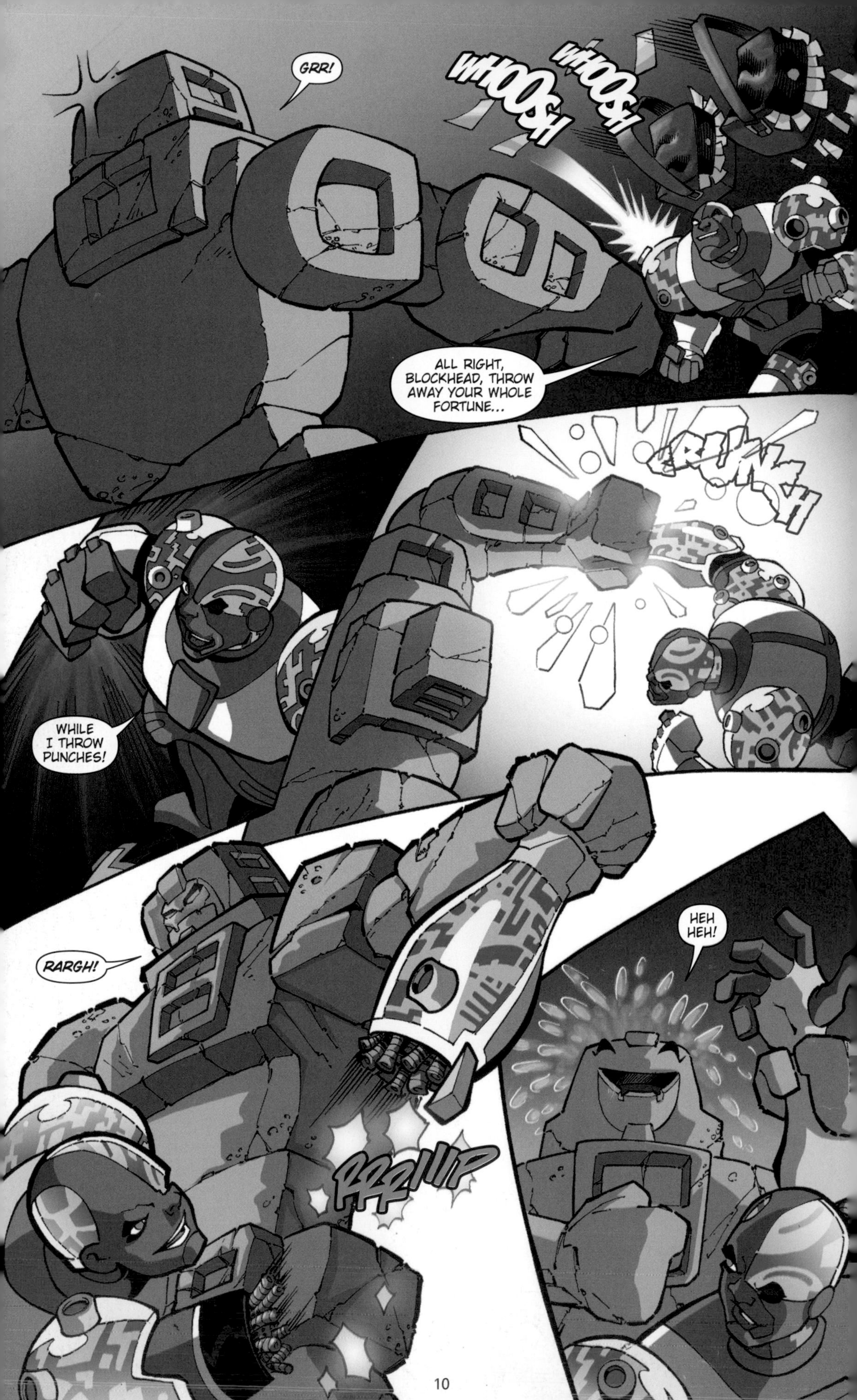
GRR!
WHOOSH
WHOOSH
ALL RIGHT, BLOCKHEAD, THROW AWAY YOUR WHOLE FORTUNE...
CRUNCH
WHILE I THROW PUNCHES!
RARGH!
RRRIIIIP
HEH HEH!

LAUGH IT UP, YA *CONCRETE CREEP*... I *MEANT* TO DO THAT!

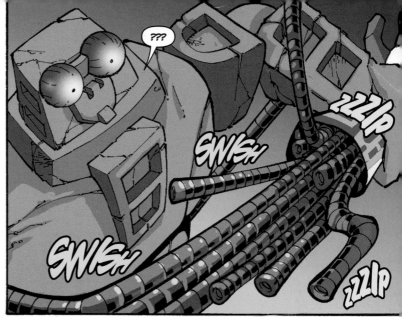

???

SWISH

SWISH

ZZZIP

ZZZIP

NOW, IF I COULD JUST HAVE THAT BACK!

YANK

KER-RASH

THANKS, *CYBORG!* WE'LL TAKE IT FROM HERE.

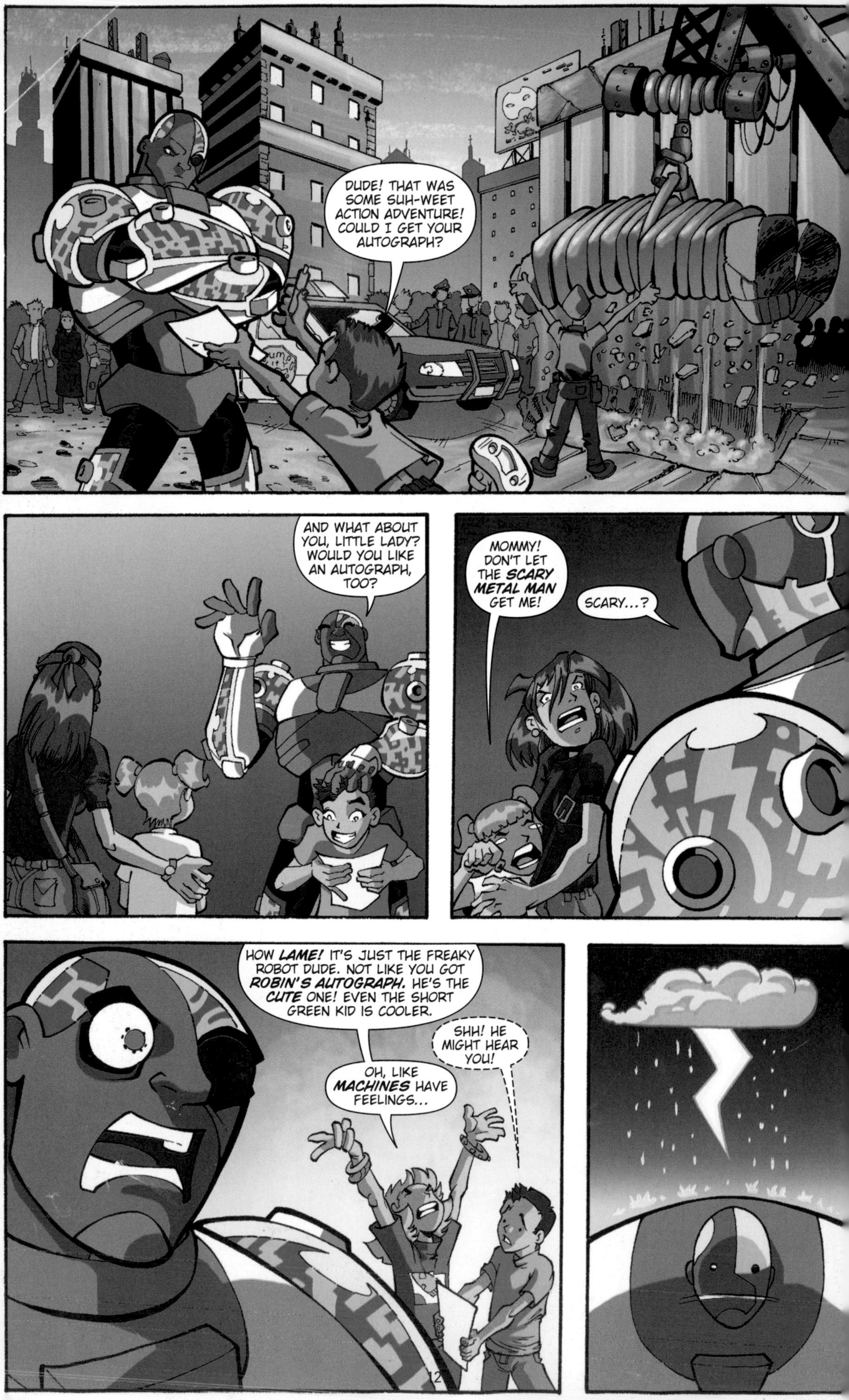
DUDE! THAT WAS SOME SUH-WEET ACTION ADVENTURE! COULD I GET YOUR AUTOGRAPH?
AND WHAT ABOUT YOU, LITTLE LADY? WOULD YOU LIKE AN AUTOGRAPH, TOO?
MOMMY! DON'T LET THE **SCARY METAL MAN** GET ME!
SCARY...?
HOW **LAME!** IT'S JUST THE FREAKY ROBOT DUDE. NOT LIKE YOU GOT **ROBIN'S AUTOGRAPH.** HE'S THE **CUTE** ONE! EVEN THE SHORT GREEN KID IS COOLER.
SHH! HE MIGHT HEAR YOU!
OH, LIKE **MACHINES** HAVE FEELINGS...

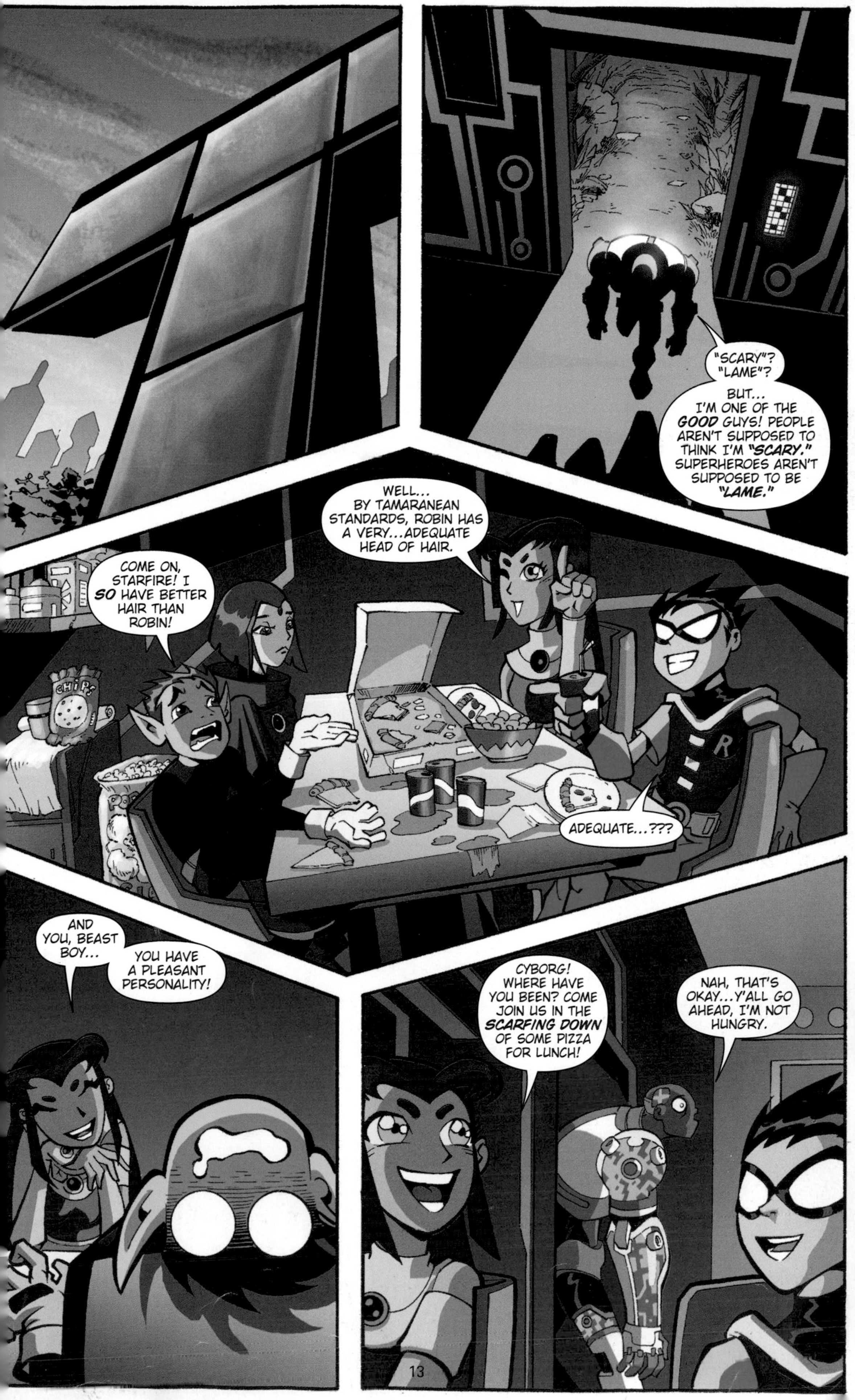

"SCARY"? "LAME"?
BUT... I'M ONE OF THE GOOD GUYS! PEOPLE AREN'T SUPPOSED TO THINK I'M "SCARY." SUPERHEROES AREN'T SUPPOSED TO BE "LAME."
WELL... BY TAMARANEAN STANDARDS, ROBIN HAS A VERY...ADEQUATE HEAD OF HAIR.
COME ON, STARFIRE! I SO HAVE BETTER HAIR THAN ROBIN!
ADEQUATE...???
AND YOU, BEAST BOY...
YOU HAVE A PLEASANT PERSONALITY!
CYBORG! WHERE HAVE YOU BEEN? COME JOIN US IN THE SCARFING DOWN OF SOME PIZZA FOR LUNCH!
NAH, THAT'S OKAY...Y'ALL GO AHEAD, I'M NOT HUNGRY.

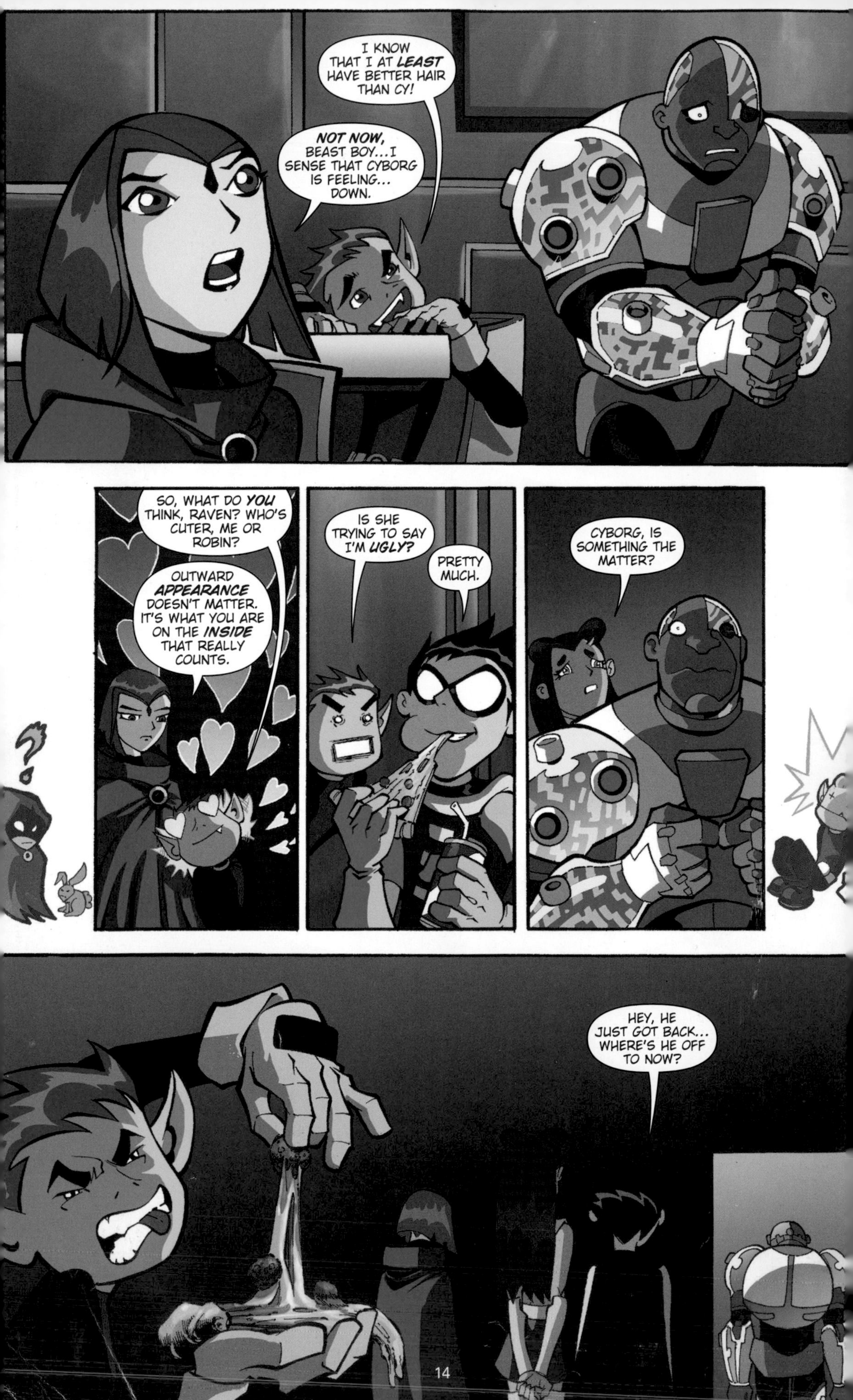
I KNOW THAT I AT LEAST HAVE BETTER HAIR THAN CY!
NOT NOW, BEAST BOY...I SENSE THAT CYBORG IS FEELING... DOWN.
SO, WHAT DO YOU THINK, RAVEN? WHO'S CUTER, ME OR ROBIN?
OUTWARD APPEARANCE DOESN'T MATTER. IT'S WHAT YOU ARE ON THE INSIDE THAT REALLY COUNTS.
IS SHE TRYING TO SAY I'M UGLY?
PRETTY MUCH.
CYBORG, IS SOMETHING THE MATTER?
HEY, HE JUST GOT BACK... WHERE'S HE OFF TO NOW?

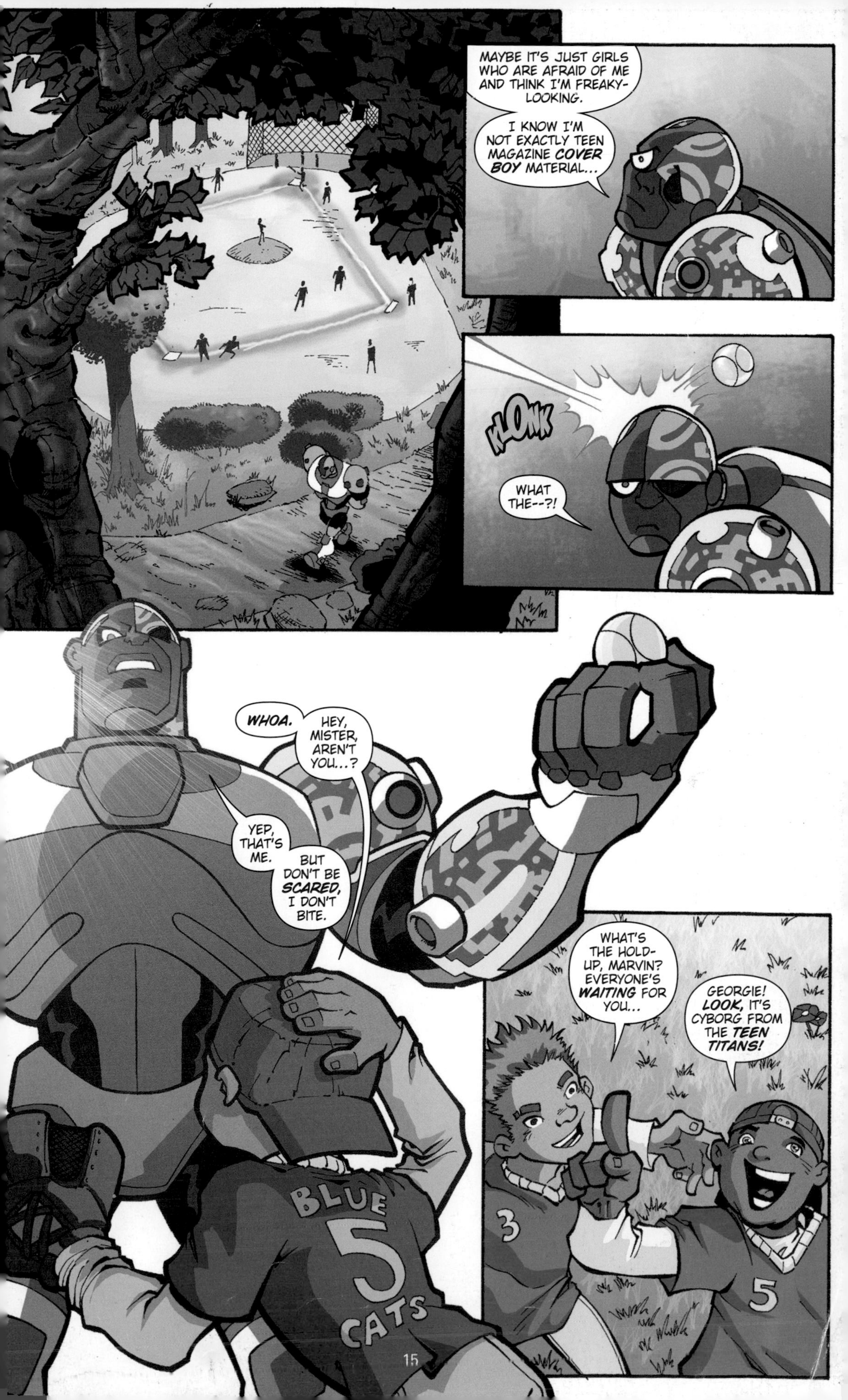
MAYBE IT'S JUST GIRLS WHO ARE AFRAID OF ME AND THINK I'M FREAKY-LOOKING.
I KNOW I'M NOT EXACTLY TEEN MAGAZINE **COVER BOY** MATERIAL...
KLONK
WHAT THE--?!
WHOA.
HEY, MISTER, AREN'T YOU...?
YEP, THAT'S ME.
BUT DON'T BE **SCARED,** I DON'T BITE.
WHAT'S THE HOLD-UP, MARVIN? EVERYONE'S **WAITING** FOR YOU...
GEORGIE! **LOOK,** IT'S CYBORG FROM THE **TEEN TITANS!**
BLUE 5 CATS
3
5

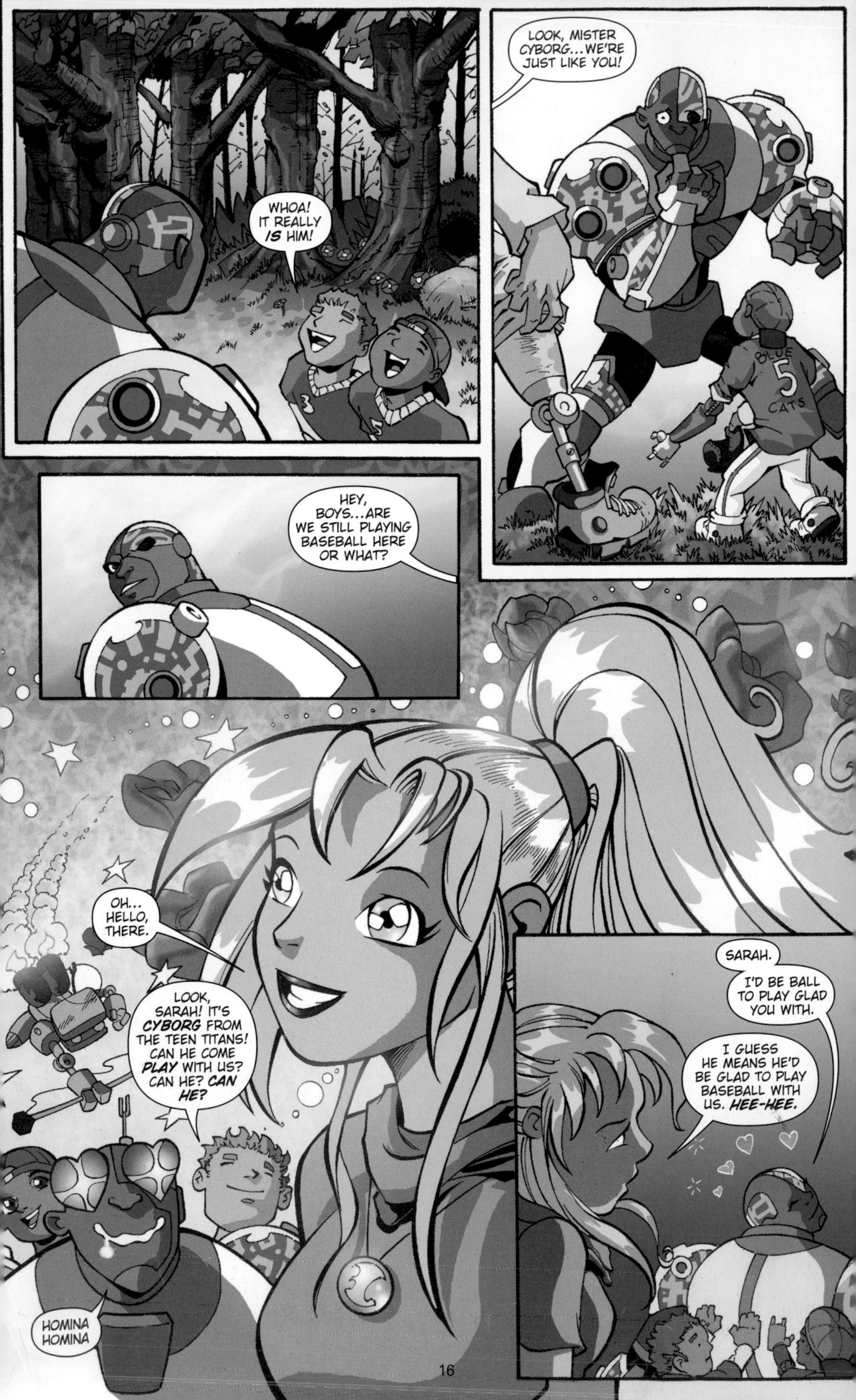
WHOA! IT REALLY *IS* HIM!
LOOK, MISTER CYBORG... WE'RE JUST LIKE YOU!
HEY, BOYS... ARE WE STILL PLAYING BASEBALL HERE OR WHAT?
BLUE 5 CATS
OH... HELLO, THERE.
LOOK, SARAH! IT'S *CYBORG* FROM THE TEEN TITANS! CAN HE COME *PLAY* WITH US? CAN HE? *CAN HE?*
HOMINA HOMINA
SARAH.
I'D BE BALL TO PLAY GLAD YOU WITH.
I GUESS HE MEANS HE'D BE GLAD TO PLAY BASEBALL WITH US. *HEE-HEE.*

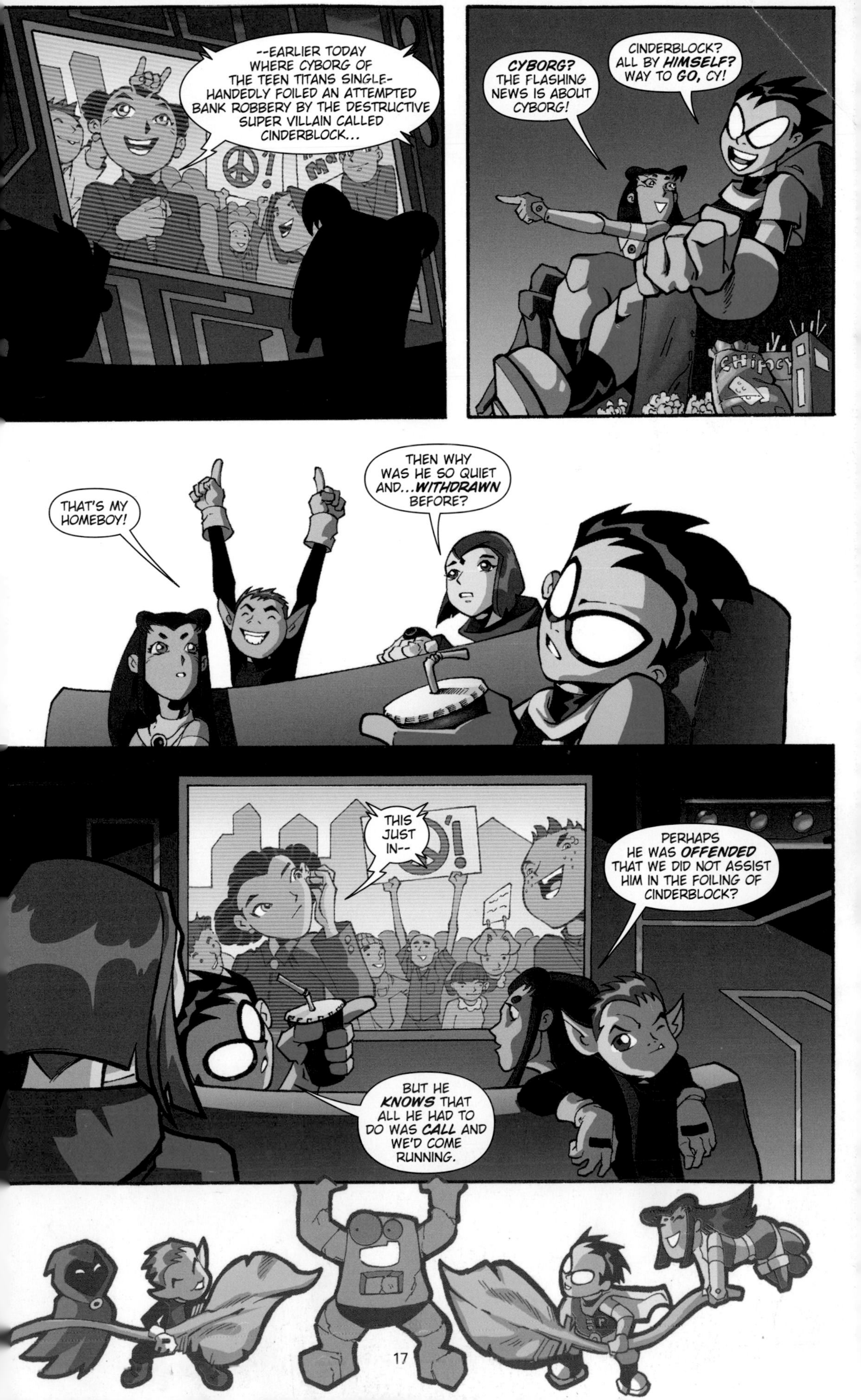
--EARLIER TODAY WHERE CYBORG OF THE TEEN TITANS SINGLE-HANDEDLY FOILED AN ATTEMPTED BANK ROBBERY BY THE DESTRUCTIVE SUPER VILLAIN CALLED CINDERBLOCK...
CYBORG? THE FLASHING NEWS IS ABOUT CYBORG!
CINDERBLOCK? ALL BY HIMSELF? WAY TO GO, CY!
THAT'S MY HOMEBOY!
THEN WHY WAS HE SO QUIET AND...WITHDRAWN BEFORE?
THIS JUST IN--
PERHAPS HE WAS OFFENDED THAT WE DID NOT ASSIST HIM IN THE FOILING OF CINDERBLOCK?
BUT HE KNOWS THAT ALL HE HAD TO DO WAS CALL AND WE'D COME RUNNING.

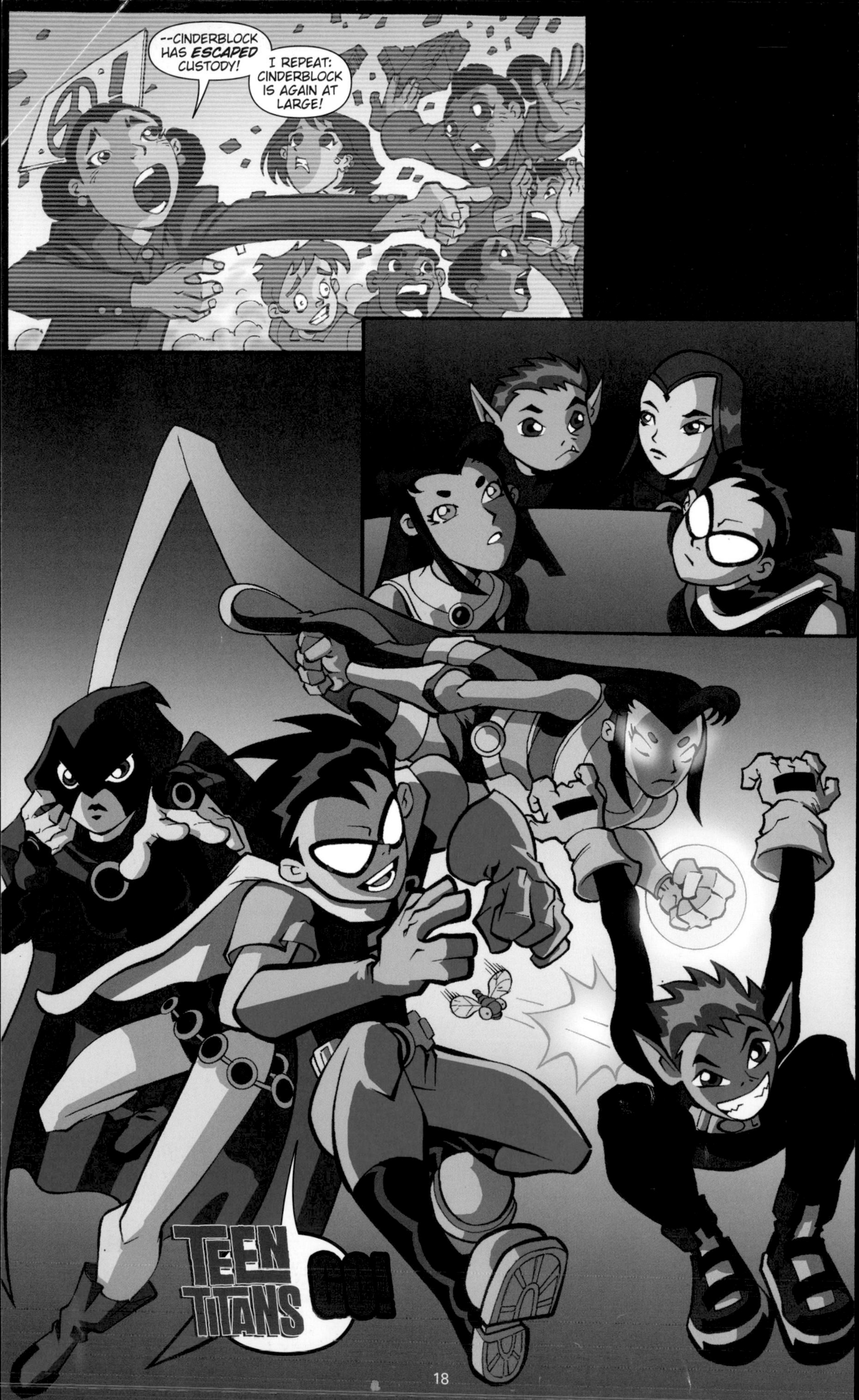
--CINDERBLOCK HAS ESCAPED CUSTODY!
I REPEAT: CINDERBLOCK IS AGAIN AT LARGE!
TEEN TITANS GO!

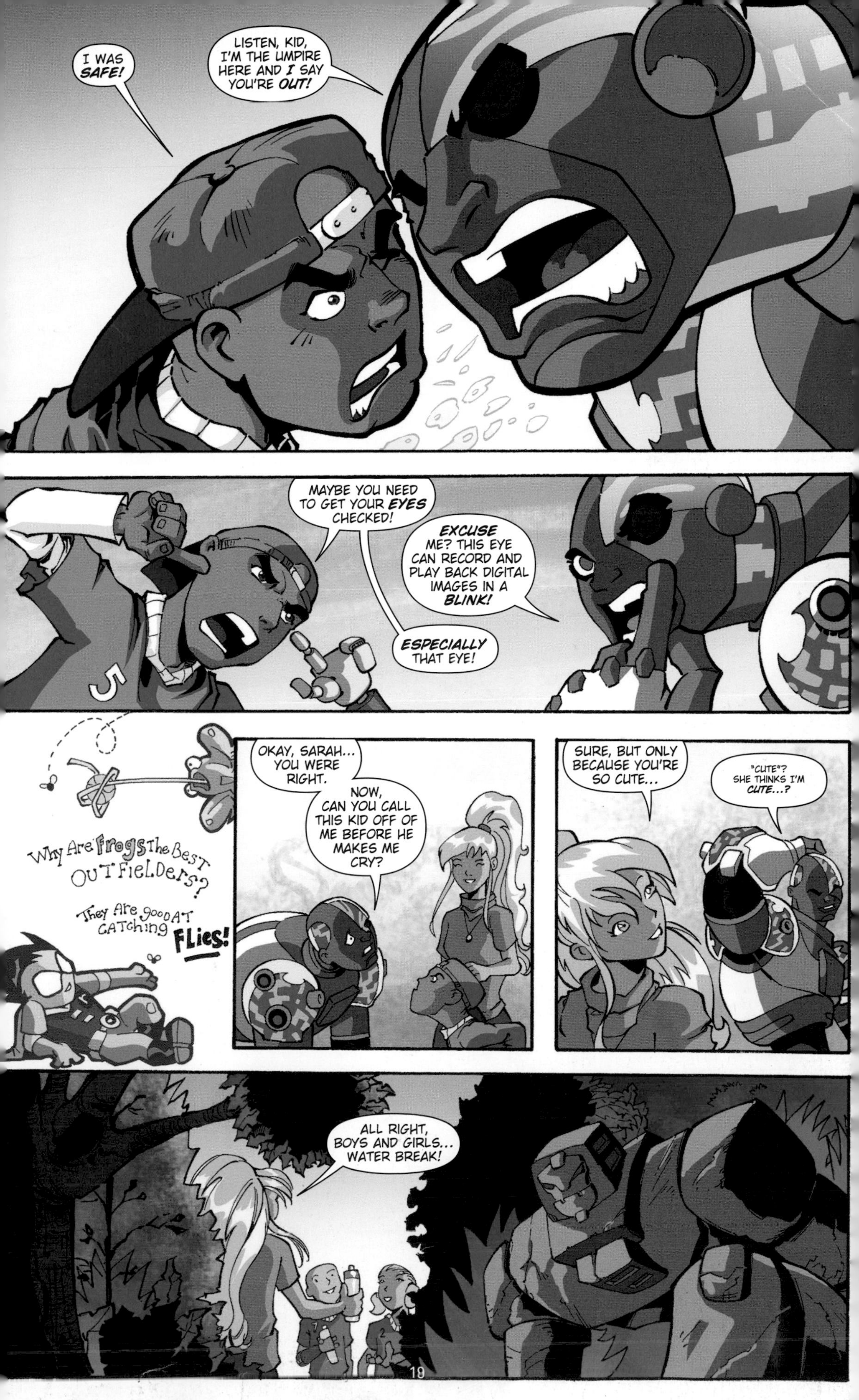
I WAS SAFE!
LISTEN, KID, I'M THE UMPIRE HERE AND I SAY YOU'RE OUT!
MAYBE YOU NEED TO GET YOUR EYES CHECKED!
EXCUSE ME? THIS EYE CAN RECORD AND PLAY BACK DIGITAL IMAGES IN A BLINK!
ESPECIALLY THAT EYE!
Why Are Frogs The Best OUTFIELDers?
They Are good AT CATChing FLies!
OKAY, SARAH... YOU WERE RIGHT.
NOW, CAN YOU CALL THIS KID OFF OF ME BEFORE HE MAKES ME CRY?
SURE, BUT ONLY BECAUSE YOU'RE SO CUTE...
"CUTE"? SHE THINKS I'M CUTE...?
ALL RIGHT, BOYS AND GIRLS... WATER BREAK!

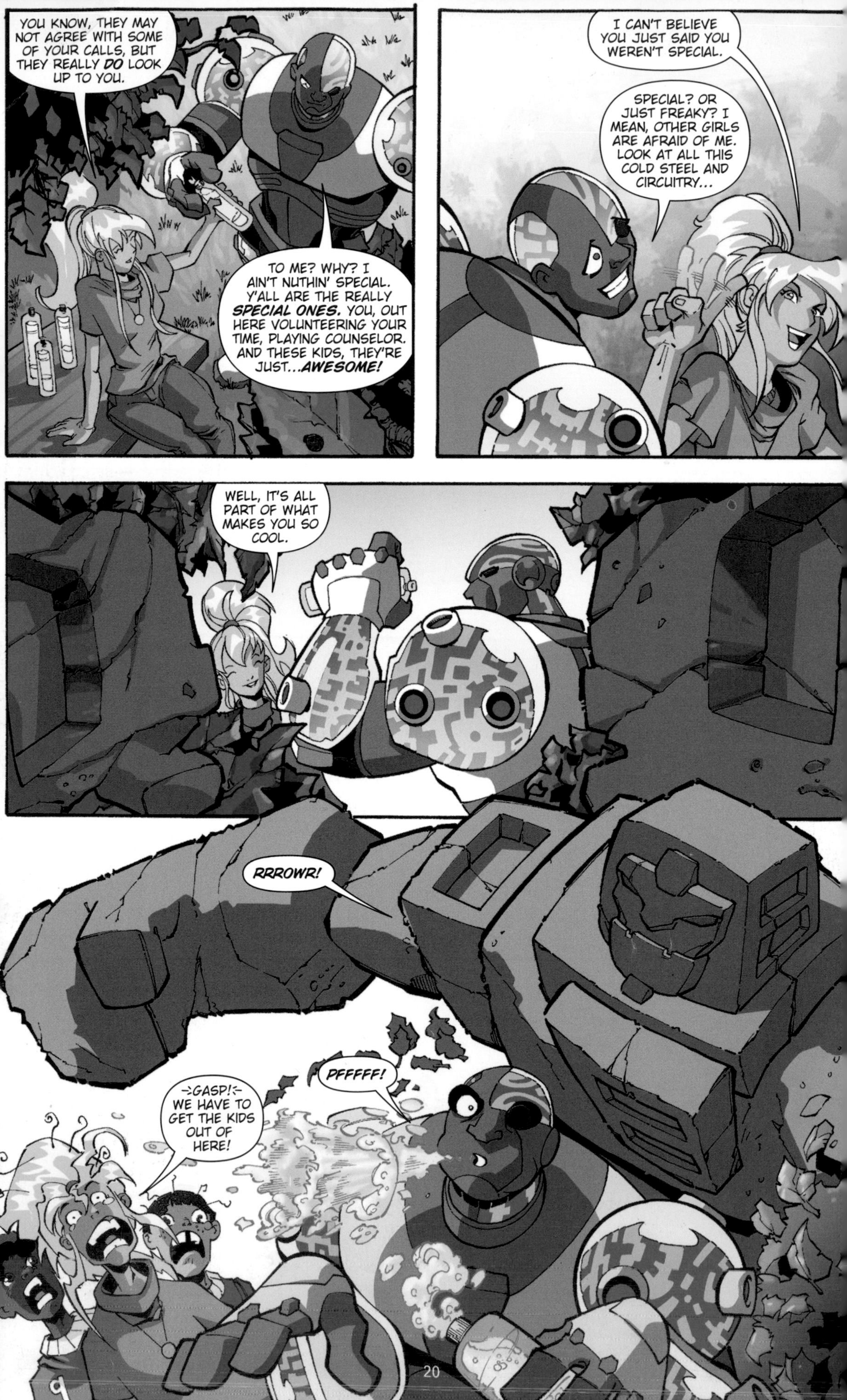

YOU KNOW, THEY MAY NOT AGREE WITH SOME OF YOUR CALLS, BUT THEY REALLY DO LOOK UP TO YOU.
TO ME? WHY? I AIN'T NUTHIN' SPECIAL. Y'ALL ARE THE REALLY SPECIAL ONES. YOU, OUT HERE VOLUNTEERING YOUR TIME, PLAYING COUNSELOR. AND THESE KIDS, THEY'RE JUST...AWESOME!
I CAN'T BELIEVE YOU JUST SAID YOU WEREN'T SPECIAL.
SPECIAL? OR JUST FREAKY? I MEAN, OTHER GIRLS ARE AFRAID OF ME. LOOK AT ALL THIS COLD STEEL AND CIRCUITRY...
WELL, IT'S ALL PART OF WHAT MAKES YOU SO COOL.
RRROWR!
PFFFFF!
-GASP!- WE HAVE TO GET THE KIDS OUT OF HERE!

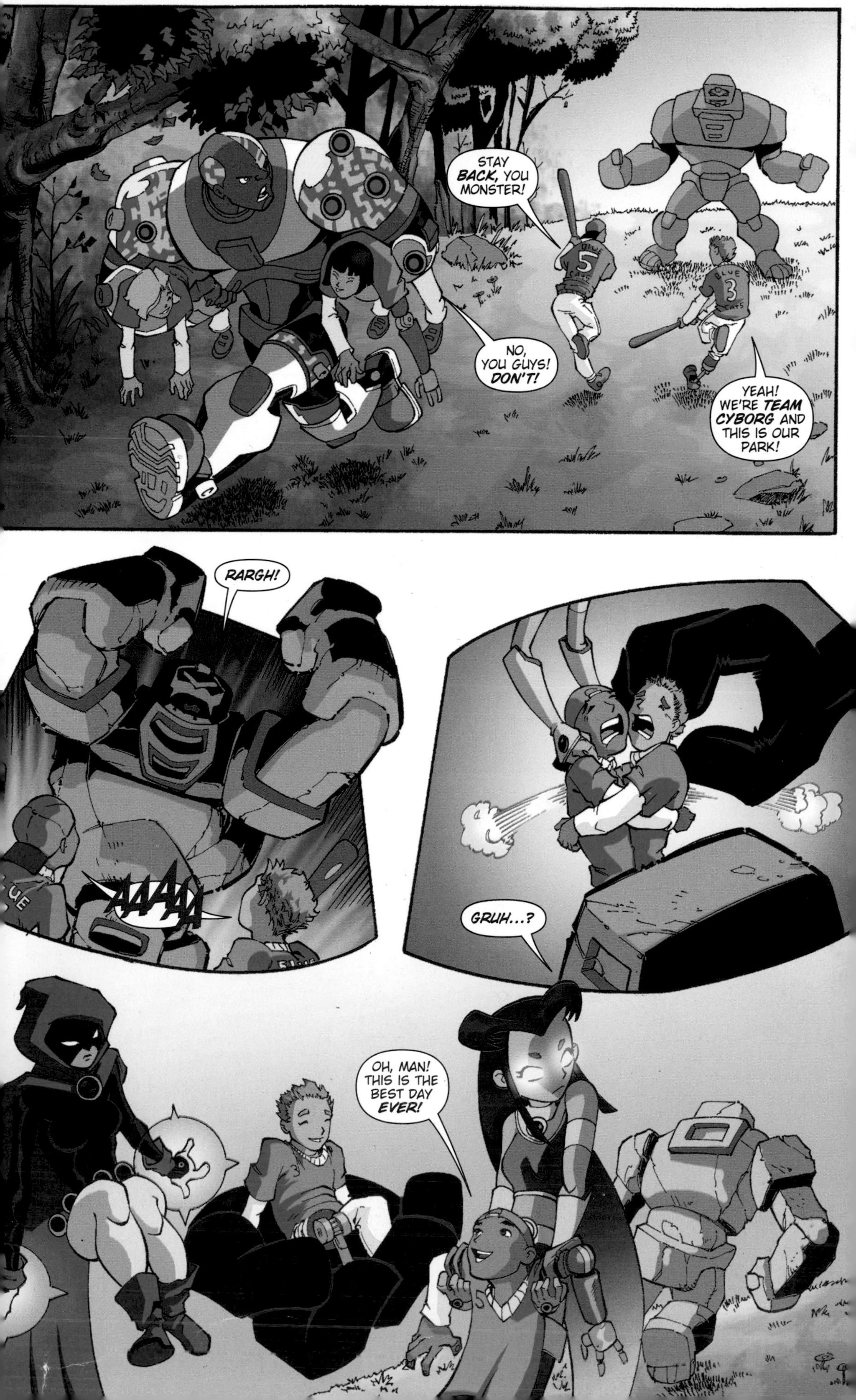
STAY BACK, YOU MONSTER!
NO, YOU GUYS! DON'T!
YEAH! WE'RE TEAM CYBORG AND THIS IS OUR PARK!
RARGH!
AAAAA
GRUH...?
OH, MAN! THIS IS THE BEST DAY EVER!

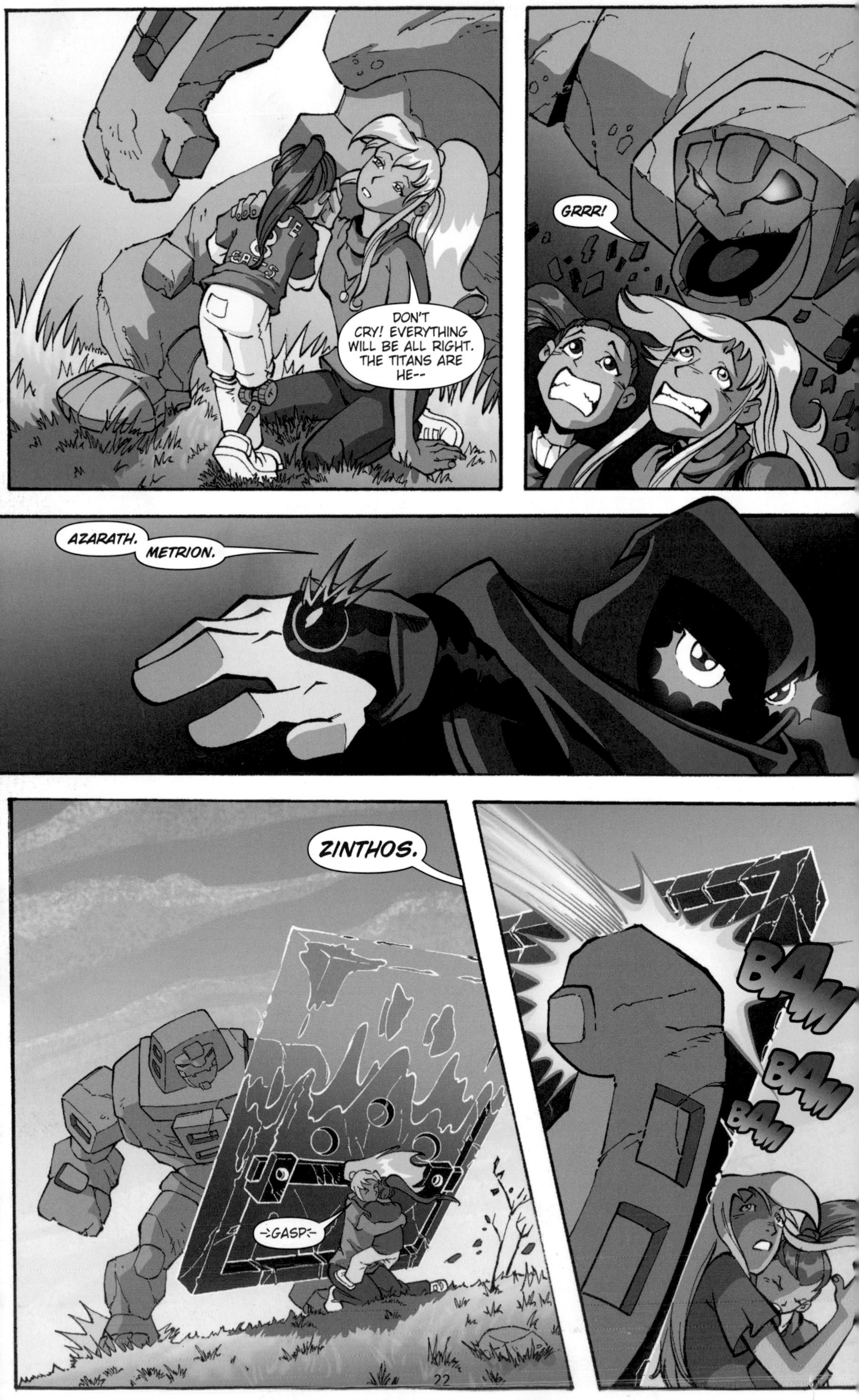
DON'T CRY! EVERYTHING WILL BE ALL RIGHT. THE TITANS ARE HE--
GRRR!
AZARATH.
METRION.
ZINTHOS.
-GASP-
BAM
BAM
BAM

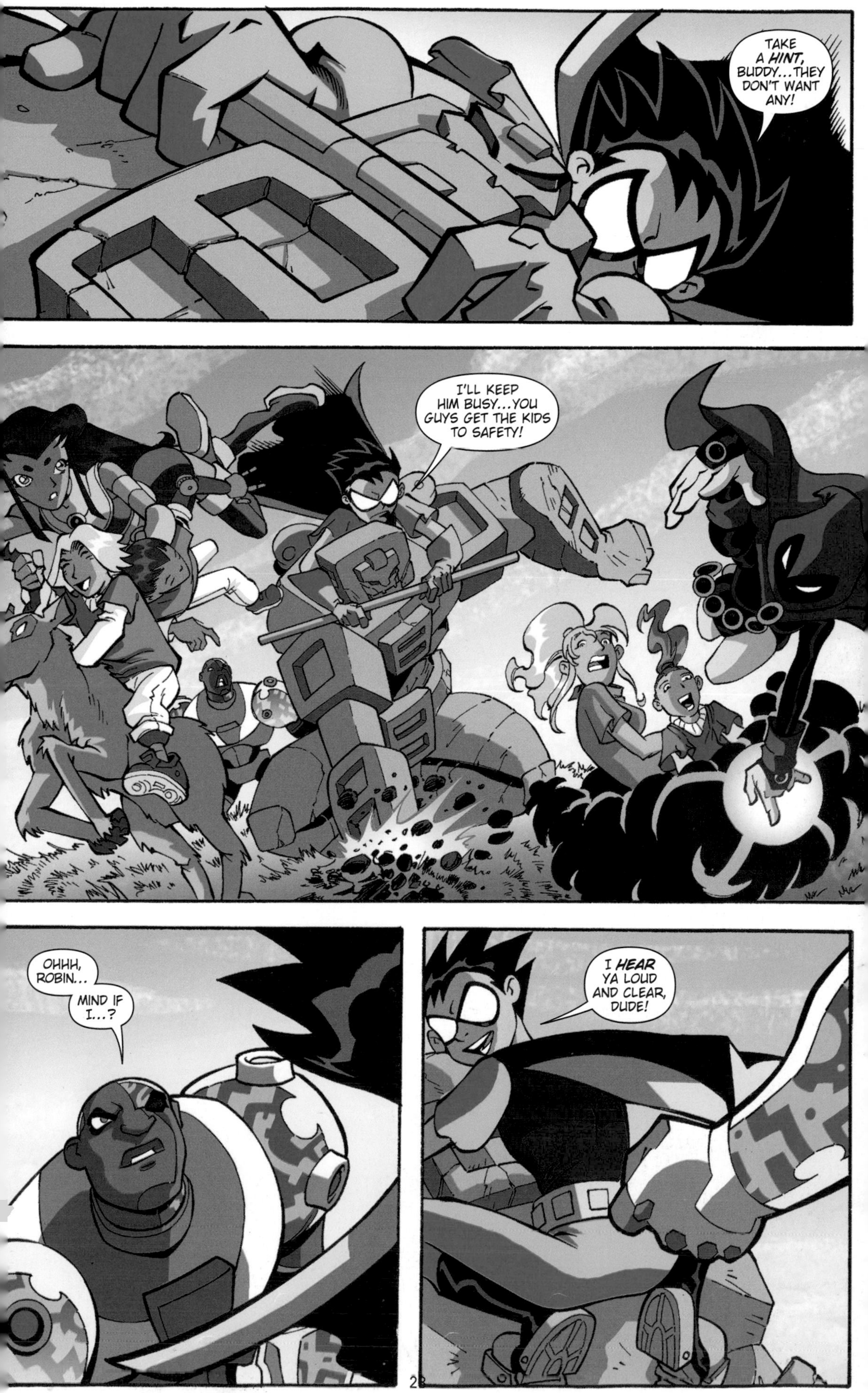
TAKE A HINT, BUDDY...THEY DON'T WANT ANY!
I'LL KEEP HIM BUSY...YOU GUYS GET THE KIDS TO SAFETY!
OHHH, ROBIN...
MIND IF I...?
I HEAR YA LOUD AND CLEAR, DUDE!

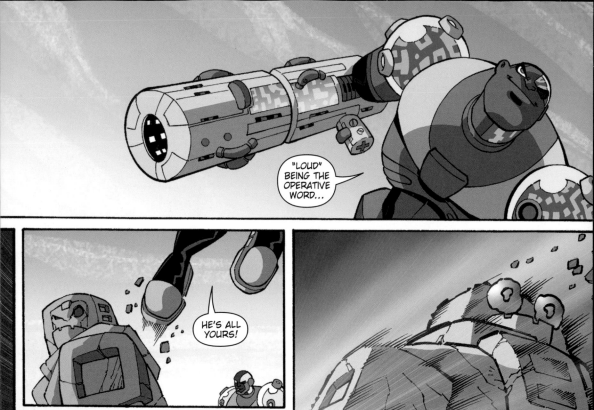

"LOUD" BEING THE OPERATIVE WORD...

HE'S ALL YOURS!

BOOM

I'M THE UMPIRE HERE AND I SAY HE'S OUT!

LIKE A *LIGHT* EVEN.

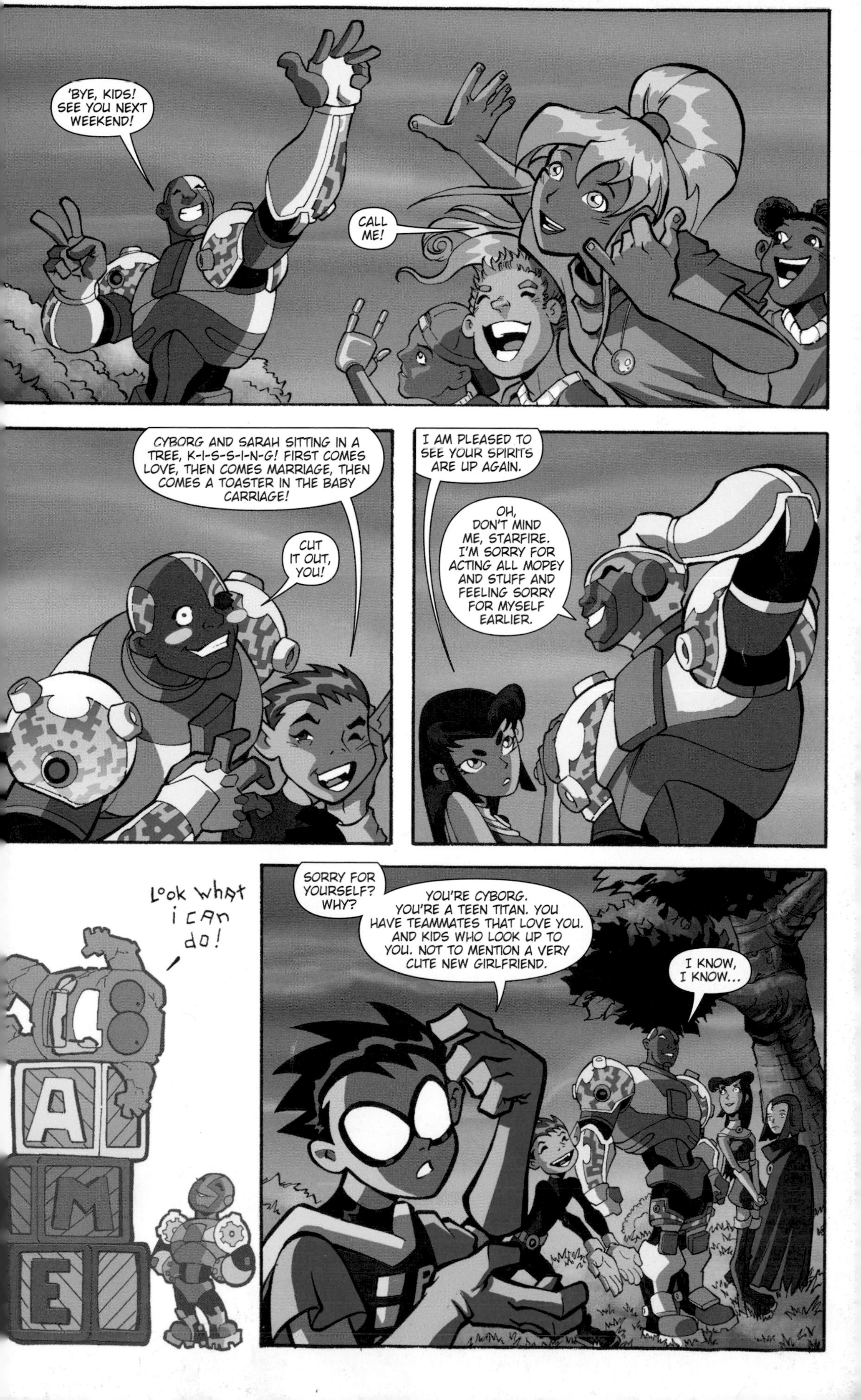
'BYE, KIDS! SEE YOU NEXT WEEKEND!
CALL ME!
CYBORG AND SARAH SITTING IN A TREE, K-I-S-S-I-N-G! FIRST COMES LOVE, THEN COMES MARRIAGE, THEN COMES A TOASTER IN THE BABY CARRIAGE!
CUT IT OUT, YOU!
I AM PLEASED TO SEE YOUR SPIRITS ARE UP AGAIN.
OH, DON'T MIND ME, STARFIRE. I'M SORRY FOR ACTING ALL MOPEY AND STUFF AND FEELING SORRY FOR MYSELF EARLIER.
Look what i can do!
A
M
E
SORRY FOR YOURSELF? WHY?
YOU'RE CYBORG. YOU'RE A TEEN TITAN. YOU HAVE TEAMMATES THAT LOVE YOU. AND KIDS WHO LOOK UP TO YOU. NOT TO MENTION A VERY CUTE NEW GIRLFRIEND.
I KNOW, I KNOW...

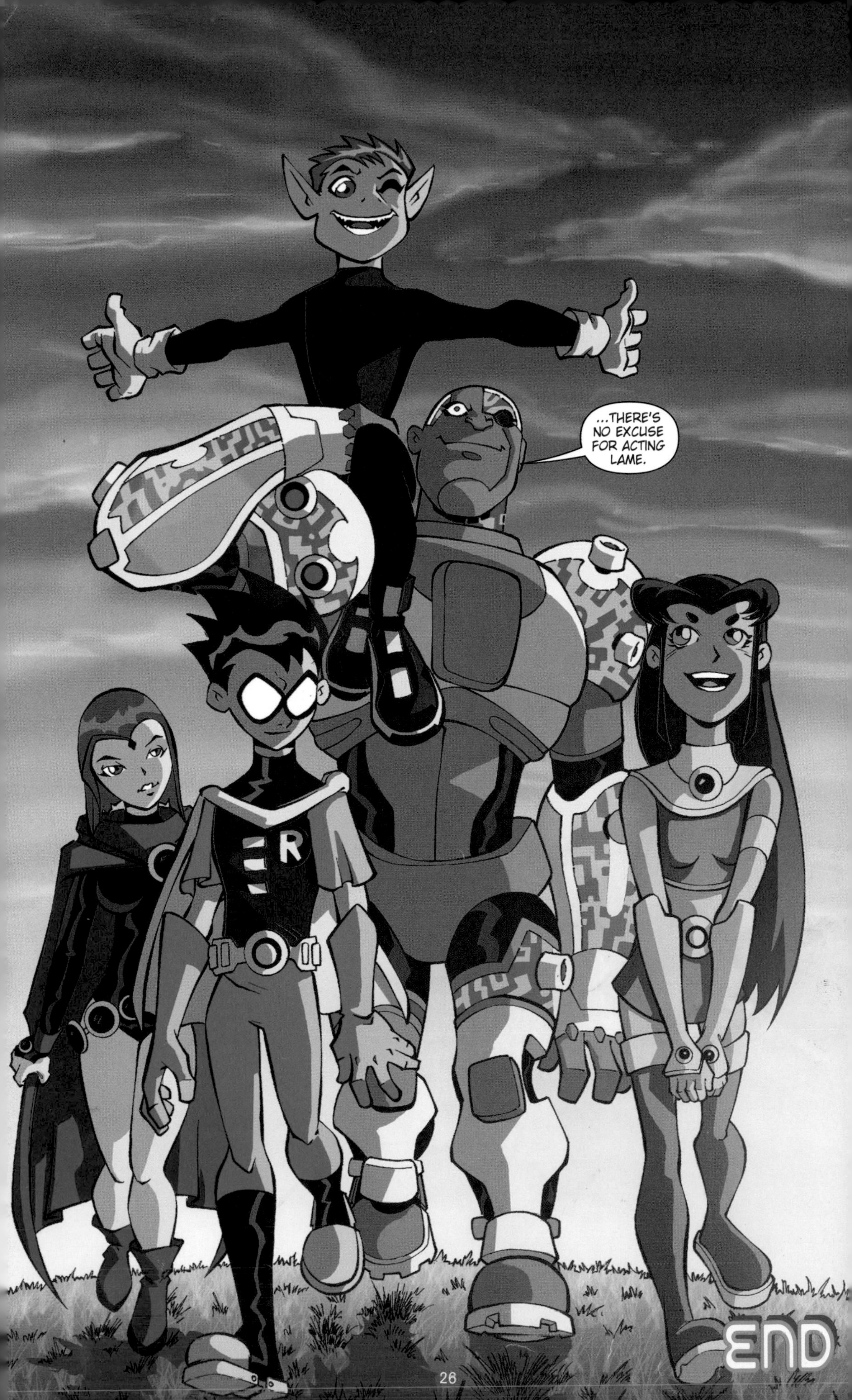
...THERE'S NO EXCUSE FOR ACTING LAME.
END

CREATORS

J. TORRES WRITER

J. Torres won the Shuster Award for Outstanding Writer for his work on Batman: Legends of the Dark Knight, Love As a Foreign Language, and Teen Titans Go! He is also the writer of the Eisner Award nominated Alison Dare and the YALSA listed Days Like This and Lola: A Ghost Story. Other comic book credits include Avatar: The Last Airbender, Batman: The Brave and the Bold, Legion of Super-Heroes in the 31st Century, Ninja Scroll, Wonder Girl, Wonder Woman, and WALL-E: Recharge.

TIM SMITH 3 ARTIST

Tim Smith 3 has done professional work in illustration and design for over eight years. He uses a mix of traditional and computer techniques and has worked for the following publishers: Marvel, DC Comics, Papercutz, Tokyopop, Archie Comics, and a few others.

GLOSSARY

adequate (AD-uh-kwit)--just enough, or good enough

assist (uh-SIST)--give support or help

circuitry (SUR-ki-tree)--electrical wires and components

custody (KUHSS-tuh-dee)--if someone is taken into custody, he or she is arrested by the police

destructive (di-STRUHK-tiv)--causing lots of damage

failed (FAYLD)--did not succeed in a goal or objective

lame (LAYM)--weak, unconvincing, or injured

offended (uh-FEND-id)--irritated, annoyed, or angered by someone's actions or words

operative (OP-ur-uh-tiv)--significant or important

pleasant (PLEZ-uhnt)--likeable, friendly, or enjoyable

withdrawn (with-DRAWN)--very shy and quiet

VISUAL QUESTIONS & PROMPTS

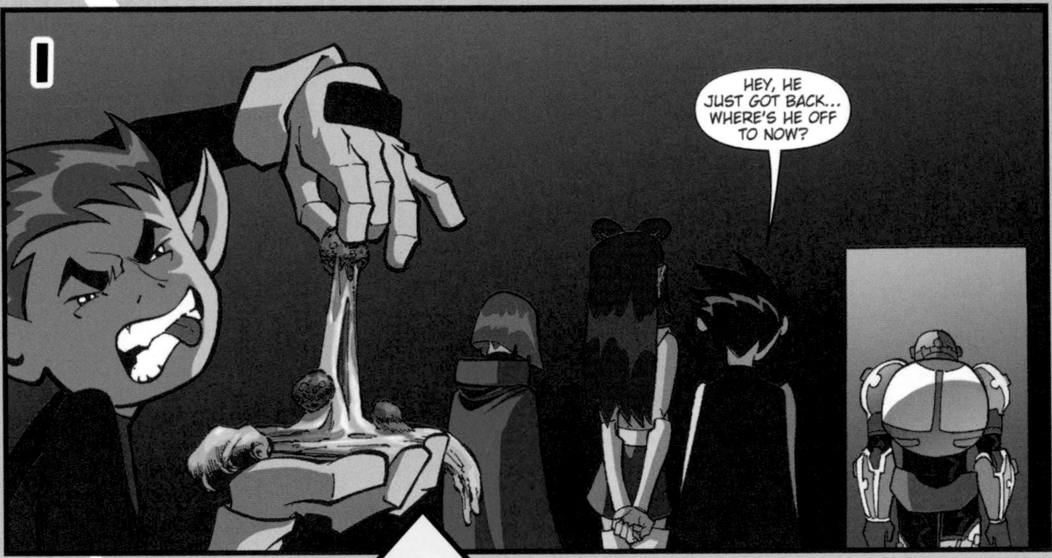
1
HEY, HE JUST GOT BACK... WHERE'S HE OFF TO NOW?

1. Based on what you know about Beast Boy's character, why is he picking sausage off his pizza?

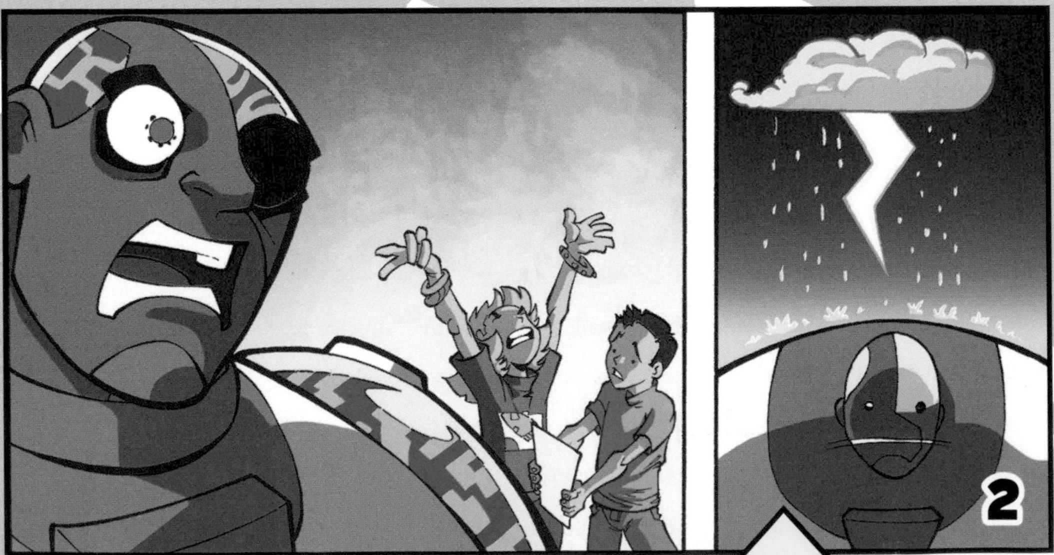
2

2. Cyborg has a little rain cloud hanging over his head in this panel. Read the surrounding panels on page 12 and explain what he's feeling or thinking.

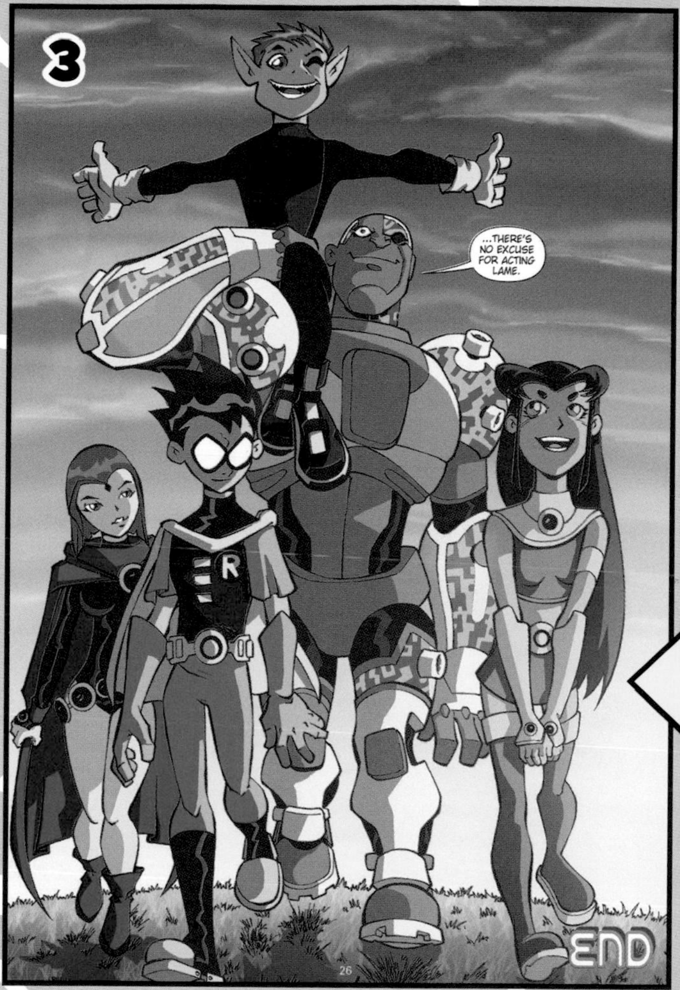
3
...THERE'S NO EXCUSE FOR ACTING LAME.
END

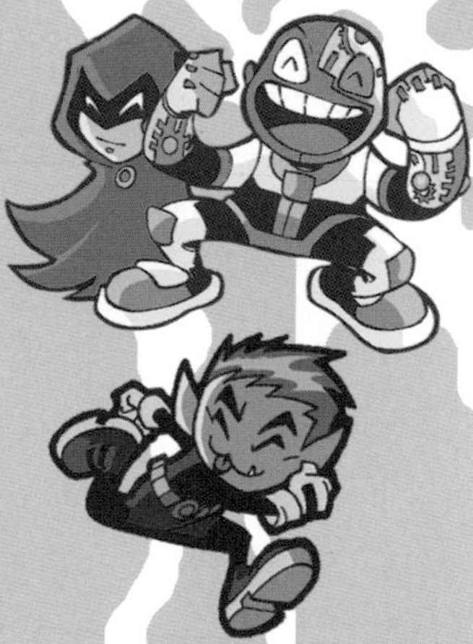

3. The Teen Titans make a great team. Identify three panels in this book where two or more of them work together to get something done.

4. Based on his reaction in this panel, how do you think Beast Boy feels about Starfire's comment?

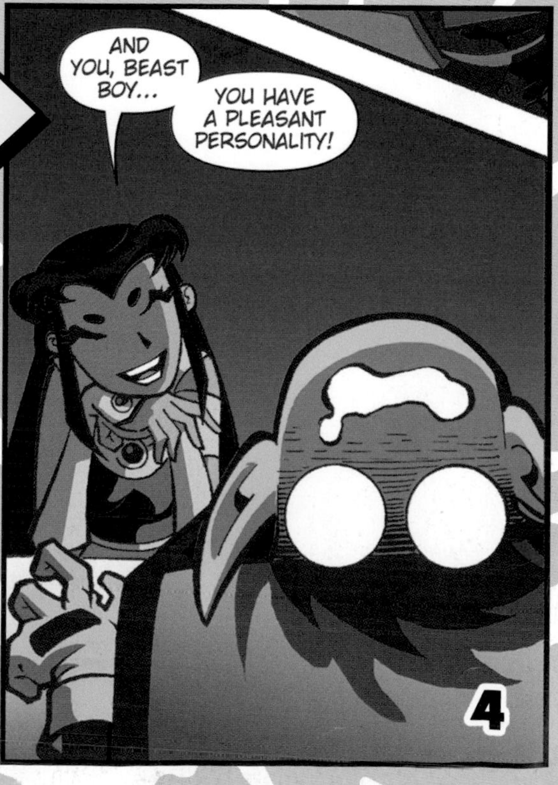
AND YOU, BEAST BOY...
YOU HAVE A PLEASANT PERSONALITY!
4

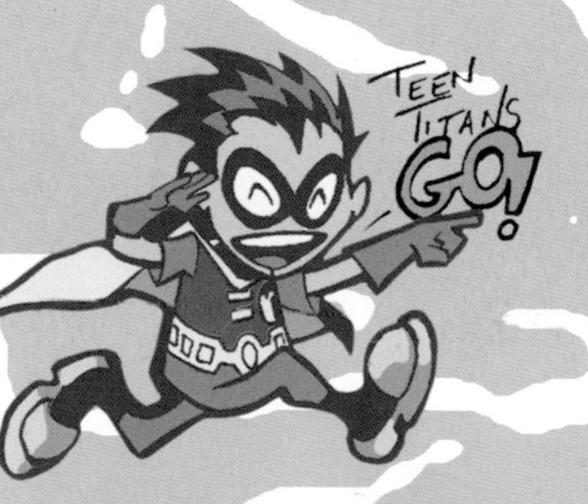
TEEN TITANS GO!

READ THEM ALL!

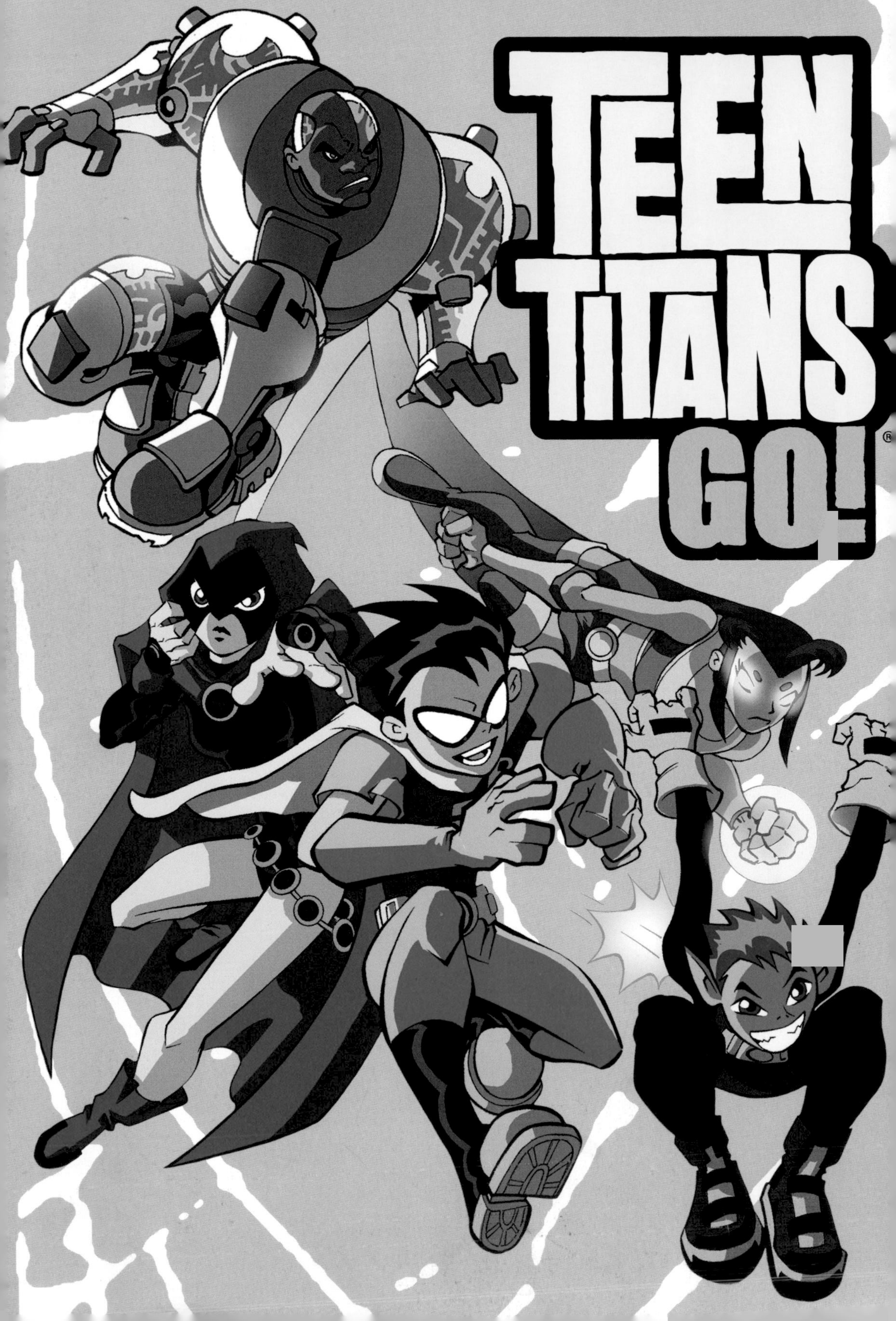

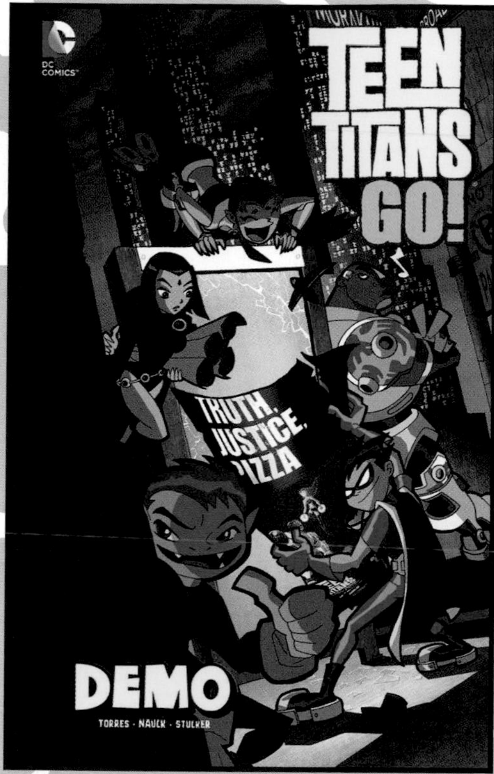
DC COMICS
TEEN TITANS GO!
TRUTH, JUSTICE,
DEMO
TORRES · NAUCK · STUCKER

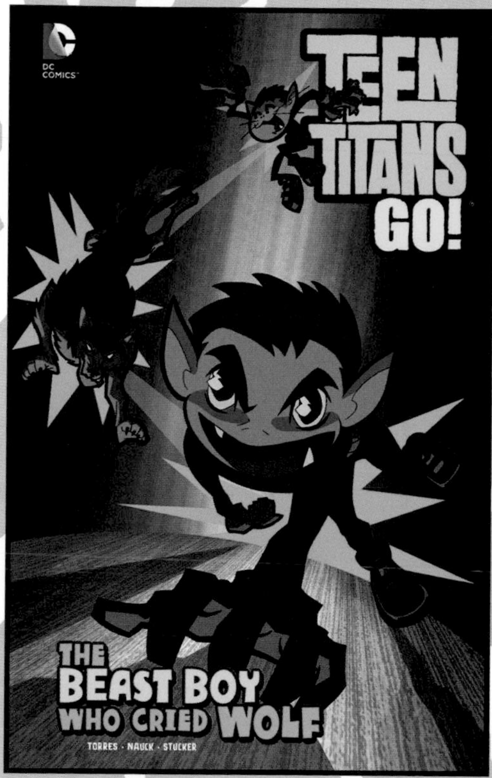
DC COMICS
TEEN TITANS GO!
THE BEAST BOY WHO CRIED WOLF
TORRES · NAUCK · STUCKER

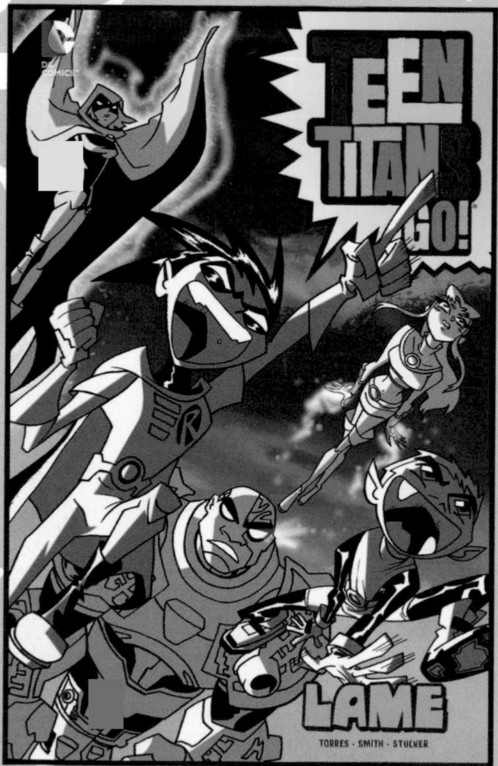
DC COMICS
TEEN TITANS GO!
LAME
TORRES · SMITH · STUCKER

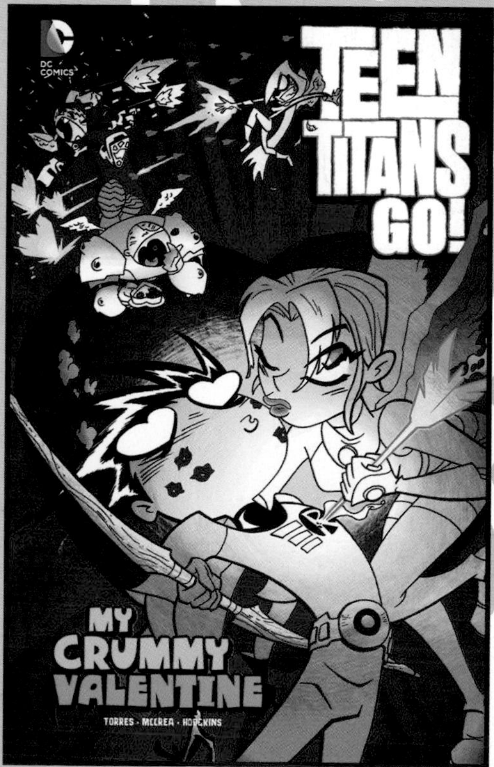
DC COMICS
TEEN TITANS GO!
MY CRUMMY VALENTINE
TORRES · McCREA · HODGKINS

TEEN TITANS GO!®

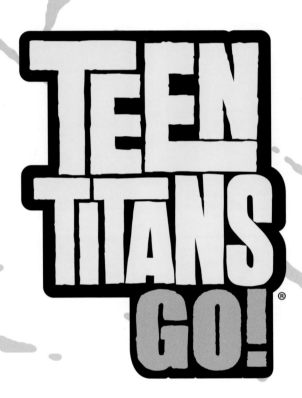